CH00596994

El Dorado Sojourn

Born Gallant returns to Salvation Creek on a whim, but this leads to a bloody saga he could never have foreseen. Word from the elderly Frank Lake leads Gallant on a quest to rescue a young lawyer, who has been kidnapped to prevent her from blocking a corrupt Kansas City politician's chances of fame. To the north of the town of El Dorado, an old line cabin becomes the focus for Gallant's efforts. But it's back in Kansas City that the climax unfolds, when Gallant confronts old enemy Chet Eagan in a clawing fight to a bloody finish.

El Dorado Sojourn

Paxton Johns

A Black Horse Western

ROBERT HALE

© Paxton Johns 2019
First published in Great Britain 2019

ISBN 978-0-7198-2891-1

The Crowood Press
The Stable Block
Crowood Lane
Ramsbury
Marlborough
Wiltshire SN8 2HR

www.bhwesterns.com

Robert Hale is an imprint
of The Crowood Press

Typeset by
Derek Doyle & Associates, Shaw Heath
Printed and bound in Great Britain by
4Bind Ltd, Stevenage, SG1 2XT

PART ONE

ONE

If anyone had asked Born Gallant why he'd returned to Salvation Creek, he'd have been hard pressed to come up with an answer. Thirty miles south and west of Kansas City, it was a settlement crouched on a muddy creek that some miles away trickled lazily into the mighty Missouri. A sometime hideout for outlaws on the run, it was almost certainly the stolen money they used to buy silence that kept the residents in food and drink. Mostly drink, from Gallant's observations.

The village was built on steep, bald slopes and seemed in danger of tumbling down to the yellow waters. Unpainted timber dwellings clung precariously to crumbling slopes, their old galleries sagging, dark windows and doors like gaping, toothless mouths.

If that landscape was less than welcoming, the memories that should have made Gallant stay many miles away from Salvation Creek were of a couple of violent encounters in the Last Chance saloon. And when he rode down that rutted slope to the tall and ramshackle building with a greasy blanket serving as a door, his justification for returning was that the gigantic half-breed, Sundown Tancred, was long gone. Dead. Shot by Gallant himself in a fight where the outcome had always been touch and go.

Outside the saloon the hitch rail had the usual drinking joint's loose-tied array of scruffy piebald ponies and sway-backed broncs. But amongst them, looking disdainfully at its ragged companions with the velvet eyes of a thoroughbred, was a horse that would not have been out of place in a Kentucky show ring.

Unusual, certainly, but of concern for Gallant? He didn't think so, and besides, on the other side of the greasy blanket the saloon turned out to be unchanged. The well remembered single room wasn't large, the board ceiling was the floor of the room above, the saloon's floor of packed dirt strewn with filthy sawdust. A plank bar stretched the length of the back wall. It rested on empty barrels, some with sprung staves. The bar sagged in places under its load of stained bottles and glasses, and still carried the cracked earthenware jugs that Gallant remembered thinking must contain the kind of bootleg spirits that would render a steer unconscious.

The bartender who'd replaced the dead 'breed,

Tancred, was stocky and shifty, most of his hair sprouting from his face, most of his weight around his middle, and more flab than muscle. Hitching at fraying red suspenders that slipped from a soft rounded shoulder, he'd served Gallant without a word or a glance – and that might have been, Gallant was to think some time later, in deference to the three men seated at a nearby table playing desultory five-card stud poker. Desultory, in Gallant's opinion, because, as the greasy curtain fell behind him, the game to them became an irrelevance.

The men were unshaven: one short, one tall, another of more average height but with an air of arrogance, of smouldering, contained violence, and all three as lean and rangy as a pack of prowling wolves. As Gallant made his way to the bar, they'd followed his progress with dark and glittering eyes. In one pair of eyes something more than mere interest had flared, and was as swiftly masked.

Then, over the swish of Gallant's booted feet brushing through loose sawdust, there had come the hard slap of metal on wood. The man radiating violence had almost certainly recognized Gallant. A once-white Stetson tipped back from ragged black hair, his cruel mouth framed by a drooping dragoon moustache, he had drawn his six-gun and banged it down on the backs of his hole cards.

If the flaunting of a weapon was meant to send shivers down Gallant's spine, it failed miserably. As he ordered his drink from the bearded bartender, the sound was a warning that had no effect other

7

than to bring a thin smile to his lips. There had been no witnesses to his deadly confrontation with Sundown Tancred, and in the many months that had passed, Gallant's image had changed. He had disembarked from a transatlantic steamer dressed like a well-bred Englishman abroad, had adopted a mode of dress he thought would fit in with his changed circumstances, but after the killing of young Jericho Slade, he had settled to what he considered more suitable attire. Certainly more sombre. He now habitually wore black serge trousers, a black shirt under what Westerners called a vest but he insisted on calling a waistcoat, and a flat-crowned black hat. In a holster tied to his right thigh – no change here – he wore a bone-handled, short barrel Colt Peacemaker .45.

So if the leader of that scrawny pack of wolves at the table thought he recognized Gallant, that uncertain knowledge would have its origins in hearsay that ignored clothing: after Tancred's violent death there would have been camp-fire yarns of a tall, blue-eyed Englishman with hair like straw, and a disconcerting habit of playing the fool to hide a toughness honed on English public school playing fields, later in life as a soldier on the arid plains of India and Afghanistan.

All right, then.

Impulsively, drink in hand, Gallant turned his back to the bar and leaned against the rough timber. He looked across at the card players, grinned, and lifted his glass in a silent toast. Then he took a drink, grimaced at what tasted like bootleg whiskey drained

8

from the old barrels holding up the bar, and gave the man in the once-white Stetson a broad wink.

And then a closer look.

Take away the moustache that changed the shape of the mouth, give him a different hat . . . and would there be something in that face that seemed familiar to Gallant? Was recognition something two could play at? He thought it possible, but could pin nothing down.

His irresistible urge to drop one eyelid had not gone unnoticed. Suddenly the room was eerily quiet. A couple of drinkers at the far end of the bar turned away, tried to shrink in size, present small targets. And to Gallant, looking at the card players more closely, it became obvious that while all three men were unshaven and had the appearance of range tramps, the man in the white hat was of a different calibre. The eyes that now stared back at Gallant gave nothing away, and the lean face wore no expression. Again his hand moved to the gun on the table. Long fingers closed around the worn butt. Then, with a twist of the lips under the ragged moustache – expressing contempt, amusement, or sharing Gallant's distaste at the cheap whiskey? – he moved the weapon to one side. Two fingers pressed down on the playing cards, and he used his thumb to lift the near edges of his hole cards and study their faces.

Gallant had been dismissed, forgotten. Or perhaps not.

But at least, Gallant thought, it's so far so good – yet what the hell did all that mean anyway? He had come to Salvation Creek on a whim. For no reason other than . . . than what? To relive past glory? To take up again the ghost of a fight long dead? Challenging strangers with looks and gestures, drawing them into violent conflict? He had a six-gun at his hip and so was equipped for mayhem, but that way, surely, madness lay – and as if to prove to him that any show of toughness is of little use if a man lets his guard drop, a hard hand clamped on his shoulder.

'Not the act of a sensible man, I fear.'

Out of the saloon's shadows a man had moved in uncomfortably close. An unhurried glance to the side – because haste could invite panic – told Gallant that he was tall and lean, and that about him there was an air of nervous tension. In others that might that have signified danger, but this tall man with the fancy six-gun was explosive, a stick of dynamite needing only the rasp of a match, the flame applied to a short fuse. But a closer look told Gallant he was approaching old age, had honest grey eyes, and was dressed in a manner that put the poker players to shame. The weapon was fancy, yes, but worn too high on the hip to be ready for fast action.

'Sensible is not one of my better traits,' Gallant said. 'But why be sensible when dealing with fools?'

'They watched you come in, they'll watch you go out. You'd better have a fast horse waiting.'

'If mine seems wanting, there's a fine thorough-bred at the rail, there for the taking.'

'But like me, getting old.'

Moving closer as Gallant watched him over his drink, without more preamble the tall man said quietly, 'My name's Frank. I know you're the Englishman they call Born Gallant, so why don't we sit down and talk a while?'

With a twitch of the lips that suggested nervousness rather than good humour, he reached out to clink glasses, then turned to lead the way.

Other tables were scattered about the room beyond the one occupied by the card players, all on unsteady legs, none occupied, few reached by the light from smoking oil lamps. The tall man dropped on to a chair, clumsily, with obvious stiffness in his joints. Gallant sat opposite him, again tasted his drink, this time rolled his eyes in despair. Then he smiled, tilted his head.

'I don't know you, Frank – or do I?'

'Not as far as I'm aware.'

'Know *of* you?'

'I think that's likely.'

'Well spoken, well dressed,' Gallant mused. 'And you know me, so how did this one-sided acquaintanceship come about?'

'You've achieved a measure of fame since crossing the Atlantic.'

'But remain a grain of sand in a vast western desert.'

'The name was all I needed. I enquired as to location. Got what turned out to be sound advice. Ended up here in hope.'

'Ahead of me – if that fine horse really is yours.'

11

The man called Frank dipped his head.

'So then I stroll in here, you emerge from the shadows, and suddenly we're rubbing shoulders.' Gallant paused, waited, got no response. 'Frank. That sounds like a first name. If it is, do you have a second? Something to help me out here.'

'In time.'

'This is getting tiresome, don't you know,' Gallant said, unintentionally slipping into the manner of speaking he used to throw men off their stride. Always made him look a bit foolish, but that was the whole point of the act. It certainly didn't fool first-or-second name Frank. Seemed to reassure him. He sat straighter in his chair, but visibly relaxed.

'When you hear my proposition,' he said, 'tire-some – and more especially boredom – will be the least of your worries.'

'Well, it's damned decent of you, and all that – but why d'you link me to this mysterious proposition? I'm making an assumption here – being accosted at night in a stinking, low-down saloon has that effect on me. What it suggests is that you might breeze in with the air of a small-town lawyer or a prosperous ranch owner, but you're here because you need someone to do your dirty work. My response, even before you come up with the details, is why me? There must be dozens of fellers with worn hand-guns and cold eyes dotted all over the western ranges. Hell, you can see three of 'em if you look over my shoulder.'

'The West's littered with them,' Frank acknowl-edged. 'Some were born wicked. Some came up the

12

Chisholm trail with the Texan herds, found themselves out of work when the last spike was driven at Promontory in Utah Territory and the railroad came through. They turned to the owlhoot, a trail of a different kind. Tough men, all of them – but are they as tough as you? That's possible, maybe likely, but are they approachable? If so, can any of them be trusted?'

'Do I detect the cynicism of a man wronged? Your concerns are commendable, of course, and the implied compliments duly acknowledged. But with all due respect, old boy, all you know about me is what you've heard, and what you see in front of you. Englishman. Hair like straw, innocent blue eyes. And, well, something odd flowing through the jolly old veins.'

'Blue blood? Yes, I heard about that story you tell, tongue in cheek. Much more important to me is your background. Aristocrat. Lord of the manor because of a death in the family, but gave it all to your brother and sister so you could cross the Atlantic in search of excitement. But that's my point: aren't all English aristocrats as hard as nails? Besides, subsequent stories have been impressive. You besting the Brannigans when outnumbered at Buck Creek; before that coming out on top in a fight reminiscent of David and Goliath, up against the giant half-breed Sundown Tancred right here at Salvation Creek. . .'

'But with help,' Born Gallant cut in, affected manner dropped. 'If you know so much about me, you must know that. A greenhorn fresh off the boat

13

from England, I would have been dead meat without Stick McCrae and Melody Lake.'

A stillness came over Frank. The relaxation remained, but the eyes looking at Gallant were unfocused, the lines on his face seeming to be scored a little deeper. Then slowly, but with an underlying fierceness in tones grown suddenly gruff, he said, 'You served in the English army, spent time on India's north-west frontier – and damn it, you're too modest and nowhere near as stupid as you make out.' He shook his head. 'And now it's me running out of patience. What I need in a hurry is an answer, a firm yes or no.'

'You'll get one or the other,' Gallant said, 'when you open up and tell me exactly what it is you want me to do.'

'My granddaughter is in the hands of a bunch of outlaws,' the man facing him said. 'Taken' – his shrug expressed helplessness, despair – 'for a reason that, if true, suggests that there are powerful forces at work. That might give you pause for thought, sway your decision. Nevertheless, here it is: I want you to head down to a town called El Dorado, scour the area for this band of ruffians, get my granddaughter out of their clutches and bring her home safe and unharmed.'

TWO

They moved outside with their drinks, weaving between tables. Gallant, on an impulse, contrived to hit the poker players' table hard with his thigh. Playing cards fell, fluttered like dead leaves into sawdust as stained as damp earth. The man in the white hat caught his six-gun as it slid towards the table's edge. The ease with which it was done, the dexterity of the man's long-fingered right hand as it moved with the speed of a striking rattler, would surely have warned Gallant if he had been watching. But he was deep in thought as he headed out, aware only of the silence behind him as – or so it seemed – he was again ignored by the impassive man with the dragoon moustache.

The trail that was the settlement's main street, rising steeply like a jagged scar in the hillside, was directly opposite the saloon. The saloon had been built on the much-used wider trail running parallel

15

to the river bank. Fifty yards away to the left of the Last Chance there was a grassy hollow. Boulders provided uncomfortable seats. In the background there was the sound of rushing water; the air rising from the creek running through a water course that was like a flooded arroyo was cold on their backs.

It had been dusk when Gallant rode into Salvation Creek, and now a high moon veiled by thin cloud cast pale light over that steep track out of the settlement. What was an apology for the town's main high street climbed through the tumbledown houses, and inevitably, as he surveyed the scene with Frank's words echoing in his ears, Gallant recalled his first visit to the Last Chance saloon when he had tangled with the man called Wilson Teager and escaped by the skin of his teeth. But with help, as he had told Frank. And so once again Gallant was, in his mind, spurring madly up that rocky slope between houses as armed men poured from the Last Chance's curtained doorway and his life, seemingly, hung in the balance. Then, as a volley of shots crackled yet no bullets brushed him with their deadly breath, up that impossible slope a horse somehow drew level with him and a voice rang out.

'I've done my best,' it cried, 'I've held them back as best I could to give you time to get clear. But that best hasn't stopped them so now you must ride like the wind or all my good work comes to nothing – and that's something I won't stand for.'

With those bold, challenging words still hanging in the air a young woman, her dark hair richly flowing in the wind, spurred her mount close enough to Born Gallant's for him to feel the brush of her thigh as she rode by and with every stride of her sleek pony the gap between them began to lengthen.

Melody Lake.

That had been Gallant's first exhilarating encounter with the young trainee lawyer. And now, depending on which way he jumped, it was possible that he would become involved with the deeds – or misdeeds – of another young woman.

'If your granddaughter is to be brought home,' Born Gallant said, 'surely it should be her father who does the bringing?'

'Her father's dead.'

'She was taken from where?'

'Kansas City.'

'Taken how, taken when? And how d'you know she was taken? If she was there one day, gone the next, who's to say she didn't pack her bags and board a stage coach heading east to New York's bright lights?'

'There's a new man in Kansas City's Pinkerton office. Ed Grant. Tall, skinny, dresses like an undertaker, talks like a priest. He's the feller put me on your tail.'

Gallant nodded. 'I worked there off and on, got to know William Pinkerton. That was a while back, when I was fresh off the boat. One thing led to another.'

'And you wound up here, in gunsmoke and fury. Yes, I know all that. Grant also told me you'd recently walked into his office, seemed happy enough but at

17

a loose end.' Frank paused, held Gallant's gaze. 'Grant and my granddaughter have worked closely together.'

'Pinkertons were founded by Alan Pinkerton, a Glaswegian,' Gallant said. 'He died in '84, in Chicago. By then he'd built the firm into the world's biggest detective agency. If a person has concerns of a legal nature, needs something of a criminal nature investigating, they might walk into those offices. But that would be as a client. To work closely with a man overseeing private investigators, detectives . . .

'My granddaughter would need to be in, or closely allied to, that kind of business,' Frank finished softly.

'Which is it?'

'She's a lawyer. There's an important court case scheduled. I cannot stress strongly enough just how important that case is. . .

'Powerful forces at work,' Gallant cut in, echoing Lake's earlier words.

'Yes. Exactly that.' Frank nodded. 'But to be dealt with in the interim, Grant gave my granddaughter another routine appointment in Kansas City, a suspect pleading innocence. . .' He shrugged. 'She set out, but never made it. The client saw her taken in the street outside his office. She'd dismounted, was tying her horse. . .' He broke off, shook his head in despair.

'And this is where I say, why the hell didn't I see this coming?' Gallant said, as everything he had listened to led to the one conclusion and the hairs on his neck prickled. 'What was your son's name, Frank?'

18

'James. Recorded for eternity on the stone marking his resting place.'

'Yes.' Gallant nodded, knowing no words of sympathy would be adequate. Then, absorbed, thinking aloud, he went on, 'If I'm reading it right, this is the James Lake I rescued from the fire consuming Logan's cabin. That was a short while before I came here to deal with Tancred. If James Lake of the Rocking L ranch was your son, that makes you Frank Lake. Why didn't you tell me? Seems straightforward, so why the secrecy?'

Lake smiled crookedly. 'If I'd told you that while standing at the bar, Gallant, you'd have put two and two together. Right now you'd be miles away on my thoroughbred and riding like the wind.'

'Damn right I would,' Gallant said. 'You said El Dorado, and now you're admitting that your granddaughter is Melody Lake. If she has been taken by outlaws, then yes, I'll hunt them down. . .

He broke off as Lake's thoroughbred wickered. In front of the tall building away to their right, yellow light washed over the horses dozing at the Last Chance's hitch rail. The doorway's filthy curtain had been swept aside. A man strode out, boots crunching as he turned to look in one direction, then the other. The soiled white Stetson casting a shadow across his eyes was caught by the moon's light. At his hip the six-gun shone as if plated with silver. His two companions followed him, barging side by side through a doorway big enough for one. A violent push sent one man staggering sideways, a threatening hand slapping a six-gun. His curses were loud in the still air. Both men were unsteady on their feet. In the moonlight their faces shone with sweat.

'Strong drink's fuelling rage, making heroes out of cowards,' Frank Lake said softly.

'I mocked them, played the fool, hit their table hard,' Gallant said, 'but there's more to it than that. Two are drunk, the big man is stone cold sober, and dangerous. Numbers give them courage, but it's he who has the strength and the skill, and it's me he's after. So. . .

'There's something I need to tell you,' Lake said.

Gallant shook his head. 'No time for that.' He hesitated, tossing mental coins, juggled ideas and made a decision. 'So,' he repeated, 'if we're spotted, when we're spotted, you walk out there bold as brass. Walk straight at them, affable, wearing a friendly smile.'

'And leave you. . . ?'

'On second thoughts,' Gallant said, 'do it now.' Outside the Last Chance the moustachioed man had turned towards them, eyes glinting. 'Walk towards them, nice and easy, kick a few stones, get their attention without threatening.'

Yet still Lake hesitated, face troubled, reluctant to leave Gallant.

'Do it,' Gallant insisted. He grasped the older man's shoulders, turned him bodily and gave him a hard push.

'Damn it. . .

But Gallant was gone.

He knew guns, handled them well, but as a rule

liked time to take aim. Fast thinking had led to the belief that the only way out for him was by way of the creek. His horse? Well, that would come later. For now he'd intended a swift slide down a gentle slope to the edge of the fast-flowing water, then a hasty retreat along its near bank under cover of the high shelf.

He'd been foolishly optimistic: there was no incline, gentle or otherwise. Gallant found himself falling, arms flapping, teeth clenched. The drop was close to ten feet and near vertical. Jagged rocks, broken branches tore at clothes and skin. He landed and fell flat with a bone-shaking crunch, on hard wet shingle. The unexpected impact drove the breath from his lungs. He rolled on to his back, gasping. An outflung arm splashed into the creek. Water yellow with mud and silt soaked him to his shoulder. Even as he drew shuddering breaths, above him a dark figure appeared, silhouetted against lighter, moonlit skies. A flash of silver as a six-gun was levelled. Then a crack and a bloom of orange flame. A bullet hit the shingle. Stones were needles pricking Gallant's face. He rolled again, and again, but now space had gone. The last evasive twist of his body saw him plunge into the water as another flash lit the night and a bullet tugged at his boot.

Then Gallant was caught by the current. The water, shallow at first but fast running, dragged him over the bed of rocks, then out to where there was no bottom to touch.

His first instinct was to fight it, to swim, to thrash

madly and pull himself back to the bank. But that act of desperation would prove fatal. Even above the hiss of the rushing water he heard the deadly sound of another shot, and knew that crawling out of the water like a drowning animal would seal his fate. He would die there, and if he died, then the kidnapped Melody Lake. . . .

Born Gallant lifted his face. He twisted, looked towards the bank; reared up, stared with eyes bulging as if in terror, opened his mouth wide. It was intended to look like a scream, a pitiful cry for help. In reality it served two purposes, for he was sucking in a deep lungful of cold air. Then, as if all strength had gone, he flopped face down in the water. He could taste it, feel the silt on his lips, his tongue. He could taste it. Deliberately, he allowed his whole body to relax, go limp. His legs floated, separated. In that face down position he lay with his arms raised as if in surrender. They floated in the water above his head, palms down, wrists slack, fingers curled. Chilled to the bone, he let the water carry him swiftly, hoping that the watcher above with his loaded, glittering six-gun, would have seen a man with a bullet in his back give one scream of despair then flop dead in the water.

But Gallant could hold his breath only for so long. Already his lungs were burning. Grimly, he fought the almost irresistible urge to open his mouth and draw in life-giving air. Fought for time, when time was short. Drew inspiration from the knowledge that the critical situation could not last. If for him the clock was ticking, counting off the seconds between life and death, so too was time running out for the man on the bank. He would be jogging, running, his eyes watching for any sign of life in the body floating downstream. But a hundred yards from the Last Chance there was a stand of trees. Cottonwoods formed an impenetrable barrier, willow branches drooped over the water and the trail was forced away from the creek. At that point, too, there was a sharp bend in the creek that in a larger body of water would have been called an ox-bow. Trail and creek diverged, swiftly establishing a quarter-mile divide. The man on the bank would be forced to a halt. Mouthing his rage and frustration, he would walk back to the Last Chance hoping that the man he had shot really was dead.

If Gallant could hold out, wait for the waters to carry him away to that bend in the creek that offered a place of safety, then. . . .

He was still face down, still blanking his mind to lungs that were now like a raging fire, when something struck him a mighty blow on the head. He rolled in the water, eyes fluttering. Muscles lost all strength. Senses faded. And as blackness carried him to oblivion, his last typically whimsical thought was that, damn it, he'd let the side down. He hadn't made it. With the finishing line in sight, some utter cad had dealt him the finishing blow and he'd been forced to open his mouth and draw that last, fatal breath.

THREE

He was under the cottonwoods, the weeping willows, sitting on wet grass with knees drawn up, elbows on knees and his head in his hands. Holding it together between his palms because some unfeeling bastard, Gallant surmised, had split his skull with an axe.

But if that were true, Gallant reasoned, then how had he crawled out of the fast-flowing creek and made it on to the bank? And where now was the big man with the white hat, the ragged moustache, and the six-gun that had pumped bullets into wet shingle?

Even as those thoughts crossed his mind, as he realized that in the deep shadows under the trees he was soaked to the skin and shivering in the cooling night air, a movement caught his eye. Over centuries the roots of the cottonwoods had intertwined in the dark earth to create the hard bank that forced the creek to change course. In the moonlight on the outer rim of that ox-bow a horseman was out in the open and riding, walking his mount as close to the bank as he dared. They were some distance away. The horse's breath was visible as plumes of white vapour, the mist from its warm body rising in a thin cloud about the rider. The man's face was hidden by the white hat; he was leaning out of the saddle, holding tight to the horn as he stared down at the rushing water.

Waste of time, Gallant thought, and despite the pain he managed a crooked grin. *Need more than half a dozen bullets and an axe to put paid to an English aristocrat, don't you know.* Yet as he watched the gunman give up the search, slap a thigh in frustration and wheel his horse away from the creek and back towards the trail, Gallant was piecing together what must have happened, and thanking his lucky stars.

All the bullets had missed their mark, and he had made his escape downstream because over the years he had become proficient in the art of playing possum – though never before had he done it in deep water. Was that still playing possum, or something else entirely, something fishy? Again the grin, this time terminating in a wince. As for the damage to his head, his skull had not been split by a fiend with an axe, he must have been spun by the current and driven head first into a drifting log from which branches had broken to leave jagged stumps. After that. . . ? Well, a dying man, whether aristocrat or peasant, will fight for survival even if barely conscious.

He remembered rolling on to his back when the blow struck. Once out of the narrow ravine into which he had tumbled, the creek widened considerably. It was possible the current had relented, nudged him for a second time against the floating log and he had worked his way along it, dragging himself hand over hand along its slippery length and so all the way to the bank.

He would never know. It didn't matter anyway. The concern was where to now, and how to get there.

With difficulty, Gallant climbed to his feet. His head spun. He wobbled, took a step to regain his balance, planted a steadying hand against the nearest tree trunk and waited for the earth to settle. Away beyond the oxbow the horseman – gunman? – had reached the trail. Carried faintly on the night air came the sound of hoofbeats, gradually receding. He might be making for Kansas City or the North Pole, but all Gallant needed to know for sure was that he was leaving Salvation Creek. At the hitch rail outside the Last Chance, his own horse should still be tied alongside Frank Lake's thoroughbred – though of course Lake could be anywhere – lying bloodied and dead in the fading moonlight, or ten miles away and heading for home with Born Gallant forgotten.

Remarkably, Gallant's Peacemaker was still in its holster, his hat suspended from its braided rawhide neck-cord and resting between his shoulder blades. Gallant recovered it, planted its sodden weight on his head, and stumbled through the trees to the trail. Out from the relative shelter afforded by the thick overhead foliage, the cold hit him hard. His headache worsened, his teeth began to chatter, his muscles tightened so that he walked stiffly towards the Last Chance, a wounded warrior looking for a dark corner where he could curl up and die. He wondered abstractedly if he had survived the fall and the ducking only to succumb to pneumonia? – then forgot all about his well-being when he saw, in the shadows cast by the saloon's bulk, four men. There was an instant surge of adrenalin, the subconscious fight-or-flee reaction to danger, followed almost at once by relief gained from a closer look.

Two of the four were the unshaven poker players, but they were cross-legged on the ground with their backs up against the saloon's wall. Frank Lake was standing over them, six-gun held loose but ready, his head turned towards Gallant. A big man with a full black beard had also heard the approach of unsteady footsteps, and now walked to meet Gallant.

'Heard the shooting,' he called, 'yet here you are. Guess you're still leading a charmed life.'

'Still?' Gallant said.

A grin. 'I was at the bar that time you walked into the Last Chance unarmed, toyed with a gunslinger called Teager and ended up breaking his jaw.'

'Then ran for my life. The getaway that night was desperation. That I made it had a lot to do with that man's granddaughter,' Gallant said, 'and now she's in trouble.'

The two men met in the middle of the trail. The man with the beard had blue eyes almost lost in lines earned gazing narrow-eyed over vast sunlit prairies. He towered over Gallant and was twice as wide. With relief Gallant leant on him as if against a convenient oak, felt himself wilt, saw Frank Lake shaking his head.

'Karl Danson,' the big man said. 'I've got a house sitting all on its own a short walk away, a log fire in the grate, clean dry clothes that'll fit where they touch.'

'Those two?' Gallant said. He gestured weakly, the vague question directed at Lake.

'They don't know the man who tried to kill you. He was a face across the table in a game of poker, no more than that.'

'Let 'em go.' Gallant hung on to Danson's shoulder. 'And you, Frank, are you off home?'

'We didn't finish our talk. If it's all right with Karl. . . ?'

'Sure. We'll play nursemaid to this feller, make inroads into a jug of whiskey, and see if, between us, we can put our own small part of the world to rights.'

Gallant's black clothes were steaming. Not clinging to his bruised and battered body, but draped over the broken back of an old chair close to the blazing fire. The room was small so felt overheated, just an oven with thin wooden walls and a smeared window overlooking the street near the Last Chance. Animal skins covered the dirt floor. An oil lamp hung from the centre of a board ceiling, barely lighting the faded calendars, posters, tintypes, the leather belts and whips, the oiled guns and knives which, taken together, covered most of the space on the walls.

Gallant himself was sprawled on, of all things, an ancient chaise longue, its lime-green brocade thread-bare. His head was bandaged, his feet up, the shot-glass in his hand bearing nothing but whiskey-coloured stains. In the clothes provided by Karl Danson he was an undersized schoolboy wearing big brother's hand-me-downs; reclining on the fancy chaise longue he might have been an actor playing a part on Broadway.

Frank Lake was at a table by the window, smoking a cigarette. He was nursing his drink, appearing unconcerned but unable to hide his true feelings. He was on edge. It was obvious that he felt responsible for Gallant's troubles, and was even more appalled by the realization that this could be the end of his hopes.

Danson had stripped to his undershirt and cord pants and kicked off his boots. He was sitting by the fire on a sturdy three-legged stool, lost beneath his bulk, and working his way through his third drink. Gallant's flat-crowned black hat was perched jauntily on his dark, grizzled hair.

'As my pater would have said,' Gallant said softly, amused gaze on the bearded Danson, 'if a man wants seriously to get ahead in life, he needs a hat.'

'Pater being . . .?'

'Sir James Gallant.'

'Gallant being clear enough for a second name,' Danson said, 'but what about the Born. Where the hell did that come from?'

'Ah, well,' Gallant said. 'The story may be apoc-ryphal, but it deals with an event of considerable

29

importance that occurred almost thirty years ago. It seems that for several hours Pater had been wearing out the carpet outside a certain country manor's master bedroom, and was on his third cigar – Corona, Brazilian, by no means a short fat stogie. The bedroom door opened. A grim midwife stood there, in her hands, dangled upside down, a bloody, glistening infant emitting plaintive howls.'

Danson rolled his eyes.

Gallant grinned and went on. ' "Sir," the midwife said, "Lady Eleanor's labour is over, the child has been born."

' "Not so," Pater said. "Not *has been* born, but *is* Born, and always will be".'

'A wonder he didn't add now and forever, amen,' Frank Lake said, accurately throwing his cigarette end into the fire, though his hand was shaking. 'Apocryphal is right. No doubt you got your name from the usual lengthy parental discussion, but that story has more colour, and it's gained some over the years.'

'Maybe. Whereas the story of Melody's taking is yet to be told,' Gallant said, suddenly serious as he waggled his empty glass at Danson and held steady while an instant refill was poured from the hot fire-side jug. 'El Dorado, you said, Frank. I rode through there on my way to Dodge, about twenty miles from Wichita. But I need more than the name of a town if I'm to bring her home.'

'I can't give you more. My guess is she's being held out of town. Makes sense. There'll be a hideout, somewhere off the beaten trail in the Flint Hills.'

'But, again, how can we be sure of anything? El Dorado gives us a starting point, but that name could have been plucked out of a hat.'

'The information came from two sources, both trustworthy. One was Pinkerton's Ed Grant. The other was a journalist you know well.'

'Stick McRae?' Gallant paused, glass raised. 'Damn, yes, he picks up rumours then digs for the facts. When we'd done demolishing a certain Guthrie Flint's reputation, Stick did say he was staying with the *Dodge City Times* until the editor – Tom Caton – could find a replacement.'

'He's still there,' Lake said.

'And Melody headed home. My plan was California. Board a sailing vessel, work my way south before the mast, and sail merrily round the Horn. Suitably challenging for the mettle, and the roaring forties would have been a tonic for the jolly old complexion. Instead I drifted here and there for a couple of months before wallowing in nostalgia in this God-forsaken hole, then plunging headfirst into a foaming creek.'

Lake looked amused, but only for a moment. 'Before that ducking, Gallant, there was something I needed to tell you but didn't get around to.'

'That's right. I brushed you aside, said there was no time. Well, now we've got plenty.'

'And it's a complex problem. Let's begin with that Guthrie Flint business. You'll recall that he was a politician before your somewhat violent intervention.

31

It wasn't too long ago, so you'll also remember Chet Eagan.'

'Former newspaper colleague of Stick McCrae's. Went bad, or showed his true colours.'

'You met him where?'

'In Wichita, the Buckhorn saloon. Drunk as a skunk. Tall feller wearing a black Stetson so old it was turning green. Damn it, his whole outfit was black and faded as if he had something to prove, the six-gun in its tied-down holster no doubt just as old, but its walnut butt polished to a high shine. Wanted onlookers to believe that was from constant use.'

'And then?'

Gallant grinned. 'Tough as he was – or wanted to be seen – he lost a fair old portion of his scalp when tangling with me at a bloody showdown in Flint's house.' He shook his head. 'That's two names already come back from the recent past – three, if we count Melody. I'm beginning to feel uneasy.'

'The man who tried to plug you full of holes while you were enjoying an evening swim is Chet Eagan's brother, Gord.'

'The devil you say.' Gallant frowned. 'That's news to me, though something that might have been a family resemblance did start bells faintly tinkling when I saw him at the poker table. His wearing an off-white hat, as opposed to his brother's mildewed black, had me fooled. But I wonder why he came hunting? Can't be out for revenge. I spoiled Chet Eagan's looks, but as far as I know he's alive and kicking.'

'Oh yes,' Lake said. He paused. 'Chet Eagan,' he said, 'is the man who has taken Melody on a long ride to El Dorado. That's a fact. There were witnesses.'

Gallant whistled softly through his teeth, and in the heat of that room his blue eyes were chill as he looked at Lake over his glass. 'One Eagan was bad enough, two means double trouble. And I recall you saying something about powerful forces being involved. Let me see if I'm reading this aright: first, the Guthrie Flint affair was political, we all know that, don't we?'

'Yes. Flint was aiming for high office, senator for Kansas.'

'But I put a stop to it. Are you saying he's back?'

'No chance of that, but he's got a colleague, equally ambitious, the candidate most likely to succeed in the forthcoming elections. For senator. His name's Emerson Judd. He's as crooked as Flint. But how to prove it? How to free skeletons from locked cupboards and ruin a charlatan's ambitions? Well, that's easy enough for the right man . . .

'Me?'

Lake shook his head. 'No, that job's been done by Ed Grant. He's got fat manila folders full of potential dynamite, enough to blow the lids off several cans of worms. What he's unlocked must be kept safe, then taken to a court of law as proof of the favoured candidate's corruption. For that a lawyer's needed. Kansas City's not awash with them, and the few practising there are either in the pay of powerful men like Judd, or too damn yellow to stand up and be counted.'

'Except one,' Gallant said, and his smile was something to see. 'She would do that, wouldn't she? Melody Lake, feisty little lawyer with the dark beauty of a Broadway star and with more courage in her little finger than most strong men. But now you tell me she's been taken out of the game, which means the Eagans must be on Judd's payroll. If things stay as they are – Melody hogtied, a herd of cowardly lawyers hiding their faces – this Emerson Judd is home and dry.'

'You'll appreciate,' Lake said, 'that even as a loyal citizen of Kansas, that big picture is of little interest to me.'

'For sure. Priorities and all that. Get the young woman home safe and sound. The beauty of it is it's one of those two birds, one stone situations: freedom for Melody, Emerson Judd with a fight on his hands.'

'Unless all the fight's been taken out of that young woman,' Frank Lake said, his face clouded with doubt. 'But will you do it? Ride south to El Dorado? One man up against – hell, even if you can find her I'm visualizing some remote outlaw stronghold, twenty-four-hour lookouts, Lord knows how many armed men in the encampment.'

Karl Danson had been watching, and listening. Now he doffed Gallant's hat, spun it on a finger. 'I think your friend's exaggerating. To hold one young woman all that's needed is a cabin, a stout door with a strong lock, a couple of armed men.' He shrugged.

'Of course, I could be wrong – and if you're game, Gallant, you might appreciate some armed assistance, from a man not known for gentle persuasion.'

Deliberately Gallant turned his gaze to the room's four walls, took in the wide variety of lethal weapons.

'With Stick McCrae a journalist working all the hours God sends, and Melody tied up, so to speak, help would be appreciated.'

'You only have to ask.'

'Well, damn me,' Gallant said, 'consider yourself asked.'

'You realize Gord Eagan will keep after you?' Lake said.

Gallant frowned, cocked his head. 'Why would he? The last I saw, he was looking in vain for me in that muddy creek. I was a shivering wreck under the cottonwoods, but he wasn't to know that, he'll be convinced I'm dead and . . .

'He didn't see a body,' Frank Lake pointed out. He rose from his seat at the table. 'I told you I got a lot of my information from Stick McCrae, and that's true; I spoke to him in person. But following that he wrote a piece in the *Dodge City Times,* and knowing how he closed will tell you what Gord Eagan was doing here in Salvation Creek.'

'Go on.'

'McCrae wrote that Chet Eagan taking Melody was a bit of history repeating itself, a rogue newspaper man returning to continue his shady work on the wrong side of the law to the ultimate benefit of men of importance.' He looked at Gallant. 'Eagan is a hired gun, clearing the trail for corrupt politicians.'

Gallant shrugged. 'That's already been said, Frank.'

'Granted,' Lake said. 'But McCrae's piece then caused a lot of damage. In it, he went on, "*It's surely high time a clarion call was put out for that intrepid English aristocrat, Born Gallant*". . .'

'Do you recall saying, of me,' Gallant cut in, 'that if I'd known the person you were talking about was Melody, I'd have been on my way to El Dorado, probably on your thoroughbred?'

'I do.'

'The same applies to McCrae. I've said he's tied up with work, busy as a bee, and maybe he is. But once that story was written and posted I can't see anything on this earth preventing McCrae from heading south with all speed, several loaded weapons and the same grim determination that's made him a potent force with pen and ink.'

'You may be right. But you know what I want you to do, Gallant, and now those Eagans have been warned, by a friend of yours, in a newspaper story written in haste and without thought to consequences. . .

'McCrae had no idea where I was. It was the only way he could get in touch with me, call me to arms.'

'But he did you no favours, and you got proof of that tonight. The Eagan brothers will hang on to Melody because Judd is lining their pockets with gold eagles. He'll keep doing that as long as he's free to continue his run for office. The Eagans

36

know that. You go near them, they'll gun you down and bury you six feet under in the nearest boot hill.'

PART TWO

FOUR

It was a misty dawn in Salvation Creek.

In the earlier hours, with the moon long gone, Frank Lake had downed a last strong drink to ward off the cold, then mounted the patient thorough-bred and ridden away into the darkness. He was a man scarce believing his luck, bearing with him as he did the comforting news for his wife that Born Gallant would ride south in the hazardous search for their granddaughter, Melody.

Karl Danson owned a one-storey barn on a scrap of land to the east of his isolated house. Born Gallant had collected his roan from the Last Chance's hitch rail and walked it up the trail to the ramshackle building. It was where Danson stabled his muscular black gelding. After seeing his roan fed and watered and the two horses together in the roomy stall at the back of the building, Gallant had snatched a couple of hours sleep – wedged between bales of straw, itching, and with the ripe scent of past and recent horse droppings carrying him, in uneasy dreams, from genteel trotting along London's Rotten Row to desperate rides on a succession of ragged ponies down the slopes of the Khyber Pass.

Rested but by no means wide awake, he'd emerged shivering on to the rough trail and walked twenty yards to eat a greasy fried breakfast with Danson in the cramped living room, the stone fire-grate's dying embers keeping the cold at bay.

'We'll need stores,' Danson said, chewing.

'And two mules to carry 'em, if your bulk's anything to go by.'

'A skinny feller like you eats twice as much.'

'Three mules then,' Gallant said, grinning as he unwound the bandage from his head, screwed it into a red-stained ball. 'Trouble is in my brief visits to this hell hole I've not seen a general store.'

'Up the hill. But forget the mules, and the jokes. Saddle-bags will carry all we need.'

'And we pick up the rest on the way,' Gallant said, nodding. 'The way being, in my estimation, no more than 150 miles – call it three, four days easy riding.'

'Yeah,' Danson said, 'but why El Dorado anyway? I don't know when that Eagan feller took her, but what I can't understand is why he took her all that way? Why not somewhere remote, but closer to home?'

'Buying time,' Gallant said.

'Yeah, maybe. If it's three or four days' hard riding

to El Dorado, it's the same on the return trip. Those eight precious days'll see Judd that much closer to high office – always supposing that young lawyer lives to see him in court. If not. . .

'What I suggest, my friend – and in the interests of that pretty young lawyer – is that instead of sitting here mulling over supplies and whatnot we quit the talking and, well. . .

'Hit the saddle,' Danson said, grinning.

'Must be a western term,' Gallant said, 'but I couldn't have put it better.'

Danson being a Salvation Creek resident and Gallant supposedly a bloated corpse floating downstream to the distant Missouri, the bearded man took on the chore of riding his gelding up through the mist draping the steep, winding main street to the general store. That early, it took some time pounding on the door to drag the storekeeper from his bed, but no time at all to purchase from the disgruntled man the supplies they would need in the short term. Indeed, Gallant was hoping sincerely that the rescue of Melody Lake would be straightforward and fast moving. There and back, job done.

He provided the cash. With it, Danson bought food that would become stale but remain eatable in saddlebags that were certain to get hot and dusty, and enough ammunition for the weapons they would carry with them. As it happened, Gallant had enough shells for his short-barrelled Peacemaker and the Winchester tucked in his saddle boot. Danson was

40

taking with him weapons that appeared, at first glance, to be old enough for Gallant to compare with those he had glimpsed tucked under the robes of Afghan hill tribesmen. True, the big man's Remington New Model Army .44 dated back to 1858. But it had been expertly converted from percussion to cartridge, and Danson's Henry lever-action repeating rifle was the 1860 model and so only six years older than Gallant's weapon and taking the same .44 cartridges.

Danson carried the supplies downhill in a gunny-sack draped across his saddle fork, and they were split between the two men's saddlebags in the reeking gloom of the barn – a place Gallant now fondly thought of as his bedroom. Then, setting off ahead of Danson because the big man was taking time to make sure his house was secure, Gallant walked his horse away from the barn, swung into the saddle and moved out on to the trail south.

Although, as he'd told Lake, he hadn't too many months ago ridden through the town of El Dorado, it had been from a different starting location, on an entirely different trail. Had it been from Kansas City? He couldn't be sure. The point was, this trail was new to Gallant. South was heading in the right direction and in a couple of days or so would see him at his destination, but that was about all he knew. So he relaxed in the saddle and took his time, keeping the roan to a steady walk, all the time listening for the swelling thunder of the black gelding's hoofbeats on his back trail.

It didn't happen.

For a while, Gallant was too deep in his own thoughts about Melody Lake, the violent Eagan brothers and what life-threatening dangers lay ahead – especially for the vivacious young lawyer – to feel concern. Indeed, it must have been a good half hour before he snapped out of his reverie to realize that he still hadn't been joined by Danson.

Frowning, Gallant eased the roan into the shade of a sparse stand of trees, drew rein and looked back along the trail. Nothing. The sun was well up above the horizon, already warming the land. The dust of his own sedate passage was drifting, settling. Beyond that, of Salvation Creek little could now be seen except for the crude outline of the last shacks at the very top of the steep main street. It was a lost world, a place Gallant had revisited on a whim that had nearly cost him his life, and which he hoped never to see again. But admitting that, while a thought as pleasantly warming as the rising sun, got him nowhere.

What the hell had happened to the big man?

Gallant took a thoughtful swig of water from his canteen. Then he dismounted, walked the roan to a patch of lush grass, let it drop its head to graze and decided to hang on under the trees for a further fifteen minutes. The fleeting thought of giving the horse a drink from the makeshift trough of his sweaty, dust-stained Stetson brought a thin smile, but nothing more; his mount had carried him a couple of miles, which had taken no effort, and was now

42

resting; even Gallant's own drinking had been out of habit more than need.

And then, the inevitable thought. Should he wait that quarter hour, then go back?

Damn it, Gallant thought, why would he do that? Karl Danson had appeared out of the night to volunteer his services to a man licking his wounds, but there was always the possibility that, left on his own at the start of a new day, he'd had second thoughts. If he had, Gallant was no worse off than he'd been at the start of his other clashes with the west's lawless elements. The Salvation Creek affair had seen Melody Lake arrive on the scene when Gallant had already dumped Wilson Teager on his backside in the Last Chance's filthy sawdust, jaw broken. Stick McCrae had come in much later.

But. . . .

That they *had* come in, early or late, had saved the day, undoubtedly let Gallant look forward with optimism to an old age spent in a rocking chair on a shady Californian veranda – or perhaps a terrace overlooking the lawns and elegant poplar trees of his reclaimed English estate. And though he had managed to best Chet Eagan at Guthrie Flint's ranch, how was he likely to fare against two of them? With, backing them up, a wild bunch of trigger-happy outlaws who would shoot him on sight. Or maybe just the couple Danson had predicted, which was bad enough if they were seasoned gunslingers. All being paid by a corrupt politician with his eye fixed on the highest office.

Like all men given power, Emerson Judd's credo would be along the lines of, 'Let men stand in my way at their peril'.

'Well, we'll see about that,' Gallant whispered to the warming air, blue eyes narrowing, his jaw tightening. 'Taking Melody Lake was a step too far, don't you know, and if it was your first big mistake then it could also be the last; the one that leads to your downfall.'

And standing here vacillating, Gallant thought savagely, is completely out of character for the aristocratic Born Gallant. He'd arrived in the west an innocent abroad, swiftly learned to accept its violent ways and hit back with fury, yet always retained the old world courtesy that made him a modern-day knight errant.

Oh, really old chap? Gallant thought, grinning. Mentally chiding himself for being a pompous upper-class fool, he picked up the horse's reins, swung into the saddle and moved out on to the trail.

Even as he did so, a rider appeared on the crest of a hog's back ridge a mile or so to the north-east of Salvation Creek, half a mile from where Gallant sat in the saddle. A hand was lifted high, circled in a merry salute. Then the black gelding was carrying big Karl Danson down a long stretch of hillside dotted with rocks and scrub. The horse's furious, raking gallop saw it reach the trail with flaring nostrils and a black coat shiny with the sweat of its exertions, there to be pulled to a furious sliding halt which raised a choking cloud of dust and caused Gallant's startled

44

roan to back off, eyes showing their whites.

'You're late, old boy,' Gallant said laconically, a hand on his horse's neck. 'A fond farewell to a lady friend, I suppose, a last, lingering kiss, what?'

'Yeah, in my dreams,' Karl Danson said. 'You'll be pleased to know, Gallant, that the fun has already started and is about to take a very dangerous twist.'

FIVE

They made camp that night on the banks of a small, swift-flowing creek. The water gurgled musically over smooth rocks, hissed like escaping steam where the stream narrowed. Bats whistled eerily, skimming low between the banks further downstream as they feasted on the clouds of insects. Gallant and Danson had been expecting moonlight later but, with the onset of dusk, clouds had gathered, taken shape. The sun, long since set behind a purple line of distant hills, painted the underside of those clouds a glorious pink and the cooling air was rich with the scent of sage.

Too damn delightful to be true for an Englishman on a perilous mission in the unknown, Gallant thought cynically, and he smiled crookedly and continued his wait for Karl Danson to open up, come clean, or whatever the hell they called it.

Since leaving Salvation Creek they'd covered some fifty miles, taking a short break in the oppressive heat of midday to rest the horses. On both long rides, morning and afternoon, Karl Danson had refused to be drawn on his warning of a new and dangerous twist. Gallant hadn't pushed it, waiting instead for the big man to enlighten him further in his own time. That hadn't happened.

That Danson was more worried than his placid, thoughtful silence suggested came later with his careful choice of campsite. In the gathering gloom of late evening they'd ridden down from a ridge and he'd led the way along the creek's banks, keenly eyeing the vast open prairie stretching away from the far side, then drawing rein on a grassy area between the creek's near bank and a small stand of cottonwoods. Beyond those trees, Gallant noted, there was more open land before a gradual slope up to another ridge topped with dark pines.

They saw first to the horses, then let them loose to graze on grass already damp with dew. They didn't bother hobbling their forelegs, feeling pretty sure the animals wouldn't stray too far from familiar human company. Then, over a small smokeless camp-fire, Danson cooked supper and, that eaten, they dumped their blanket rolls under the cottonwoods then moved back to the camp-fire to sit on logs in the flickering light close to the dancing flames.

'Clear ground with no cover on the other side of the creek,' Gallant said, his eyes on the big man smoking a cigarette and casting wild shadows on the other side of fire. 'Also, if we need it we've got cover of sorts close by, and beyond those cottonwoods there's more open ground.'

'Your point being?' Danson said.

'If this dangerous twist you mentioned briefly as some kind of afterthought means we're being followed, you've made damn sure nobody on horseback can get close without being seen.'

Danson drew on his cigarette. Smoke clung like skeins of cobwebs in the strands of his black beard. His eyes glinted under heavy brows.

He gestured vaguely.

'Those two, last night, those two men, the short and the tall. They were lying. It wasn't just a game of poker between strangers. They're with the Eagans.'

'I never did believe them. They were backed up against the saloon's wall under Lake's gun, so I figured they told him what he wanted to hear. But that's me hazarding a guess, whereas you seem certain. What happened?'

'I've never seen Jake move so fast.'

'Jake?'

'Arkle, the Last Chance barman. You rode off, I was locking my door. He came rushing out into the street fastening filthy pants, hoisting those damn red suspenders. He watched you heading south and ran like a scalded cat for the climb up through the houses.'

'He see you?'

'I made sure he did. He'd got me curious. I gave him a friendly wave, rode up after him as if I was heading out of town that way. That broke any connection between you and me, told him you were

48

riding south on your own.'

'Amazing the way a good breakfast oils a man's brain matter,' Gallant said.

'Or maybe it's the after effects of what I keep by the fire in that cracked jug,' Danson said, grinning. 'Anyway, I let Jake stay ahead of me. He was puffing and panting when he staggered up to the house next up from the general store. By the time I got there and rode on by he'd hammered on the door. He was calling those *hombres* by name – Quint, Largo – and one of 'em came tumbling out in grey long johns, and Jake began jabbering away and flapping a hand wildly in the general direction you'd taken.'

'One of them?'

'There's a patch of scrub behind those houses. I could see one horse tethered, and, yes, just the one man, the tall feller, answered Jake's hammering. The other, shorty. . . ?' Danson shrugged. 'If asked to make a guess, I'd say he's gone to join Gord Eagan.'

'Did the one left behind see you?'

'Jake called him Quint – and of course he did. That was my intention.'

'Yes,' Gallant said thoughtfully, 'you already said, and him expecting me to be heading south on my own does give us an advantage.'

'It does if Quint comes after us – after you – which he will do. He was left behind to see if you rose from the dead, and if you did he's been told to finish the job started by Eagan.'

'But Eagan didn't come back to Salvation Creek, couldn't give that order. He gave up looking for me, and rode off.'

'All right, but this feller Quint learned of your miraculous survival from Jake Arkle, and he'll have worked out for himself what he needs to do to curry favour with the boss.' Danson paused. 'But that's not what's kept me quiet for most of the day. There's something very wrong, Gallant.'

There was a short silence. Danson flicked his cigarette end into the fire, the shower of sparks reflecting in his watchful black eyes. Gallant stood up, idly touched the Peacemaker in its holster, walked away across the wet grass. The horses were dozing under the cottonwoods fifty yards away, behind Danson. Listening hard, Gallant could hear nothing above the crackle of the fire, the murmur of the nearby creek, the distant whistling of bats. He knew Danson had chosen just about the ideal site for their camp, but the advantages it gave them had disappeared with nightfall: horses could be abandoned half a mile away, and in darkness an armed man with the ability to move silently on foot could easily cross open ground without being observed. But why would he bother? All that was needed was a clever man with a well trained horse, a good cow pony, and speed, and the element of surprise.

'Yes, there is,' Gallant said, 'and it's what's been bothering me: why did Chet Eagan take Melody Lake all the way to El Dorado?' He swung around, and from a distance saw Danson nodding, waiting. 'We talked about buying time, but we knew deep down that's a complication when there's a much easier way.

A man with Emerson Judd's power wouldn't waste money paying a bunch of men to kidnap and hold captive a lawyer. There's no certainty in that, and he wouldn't leave anything to chance. No, Judd would pay one man to put a bullet in her head.'

'But as that hasn't happened,' Danson said, 'it means somebody's making sure Melody Lake is well out of the way, but is unharmed. Now, who would that be?'

Gallant had his mouth open to give an answer that, in the circumstances, made no sense whatsoever. The words never came. Close to his face there was a soft whisper of sound as of a night bird's swift passing, then Karl Danson's head exploded in a shower of blood and brains.

Gallant hit the ground hard. The sound of the killing shot closely followed the sickening splat of the bullet shattering Danson's skull. The gunman – according to Danson that would be the tall man, Quint – had to be close, probably using the cottonwoods as cover. Danson had flopped heavily across the log by the fire. His weight shifted it close to the flames. Gallant, flat, spread-eagled, adrenalin pumping, was still several yards away. But if the killer was that close, he would have watched Gallant walk away from Danson. Why then had he shot Danson, when with his rifle he should have been tracking the danger man, Gallant?

A second shot kicked dirt into Gallant's face, wiping all questions from his mind. The grassy clearing chosen by Danson provided no cover. There was

51

the creek, the shelter of the bank if Gallant slid down on to the shingle – but enough was enough; he shivered at haunting memories, vowed to stay well clear of cold water. Twisting on to one side to draw his six-gun, he snapped two wild shots at the cottonwoods. Before the crack of the gunpowder detonations had died he was up on his feet and in a crouching, weaving run.

He had one clear, temporary advantage. Danson had been killed by a rifle bullet. For a man sheltering in trees a rifle is a clumsy weapon, the barrel too long for a quick change of aim. Even as he ran Gallant heard the gunman's loud curse as the barrel snagged on a branch, the crackling snap of brush as it was wrenched free. Then the heat of the campfire was in his face. A flat dive, a bone-crunching landing and, kicking away glowing embers with a sweep of his right leg, he was behind the log over which the lifeless body of Karl Danson was draped.

Recovering fast, the hidden gunman fired twice. Both shots thudded into Danson's body. Softly, Gallant said, 'Sorry, partner.' He reached out, touched the dead man's warm shoulder. Snapped another two shots with his Colt towards the woods, then pouched the pistol and slid Danson's Remington .44 from its holster.

He was now a two-gun man, for what it was worth. A Remington .44, a looped gunbelt full of cartridges for his Colt, but nowhere to go. Pinned down behind a cooling corpse, if he lifted his head a single shot from the rifle would see his brains mingle with the bloody mess of Danson's. His own rifle, and ammunition for the .44, were with the horses. Not hobbling them had been a mistake. They were nervous, not panicking but moving at a steady trot away from the crackle of gunfire. And Gallant's temporary advantage had gone. Quint would by now have changed position to give himself, his long arms and even longer rifle, more room to move. He had a fixed target caught in a circle of firelight, and all the time in the world.

But so had Gallant.

Between the campfire and the trees there was that narrow stretch of open grassland. The last light reflecting from the clouds had died, true night had fallen and the moon remained hidden behind high cloud, but the warm glow of the fire was enough to light up the expanse of grass and touch the branches of the nearest cottonwoods. A break from cover by either man would leave him fatally exposed – Gallant more so, because of his awkward prone position in the firelight – and give the other a clear killing shot.

So let's call the odds roughly even, Gallant thought; and the play on words from a man taught privately then in an English public school brought the briefest of chill smiles.

Then, as if to pour scorn on his own logic and reasoning, he made his move.

He broke cover.

With supreme confidence.

When in a tight corner, Born Gallant had always relied on instinct, backed his subconscious to show him the way out of trouble. Before he sprang to his feet that instinct saw him again whispering his apologies to the big man – then using all his strength to push Danson's massive bulk off the log and on to the flames.

All light was immediately extinguished. The air was filled with the stench of cloth burning. If the gunman in the woods had been staring hard into the firelight, he would now be as near to blindness as made no difference, and it would take valuable seconds for his night vision to be restored. That was all the time Gallant needed. Keeping flat, he snaked away from Danson, crawled silently across the grass for five yards, ten yards – then, listening, hearing nothing from the woods, he sprang to his feet. Running fast, running low, not bothering to swerve, to zigzag, he made straight for the retreating horses. As he ran he tried for a soft, low whistle; drew a panting breath, whistled again, knowing that his roan at least would recognize the familiar signal.

But it was the black gelding that came trotting towards him out of the darkness.

Gallant was still holding Danson's .44 Remington, but pouched on Danson's horse he now had a better weapon close to hand. He tossed the pistol into the grass, reached up for the horn as the gleaming black horse drew alongside him, nuzzled his cheek. Then he vaulted into the saddle. He searched for the stirrups; they'd been adjusted for the big man and were way too long for Gallant to reach.

So, damn me, Gallant thought, who the hell needs

stirrups at a time like this? And with a fierce yell of, 'Tally ho and away we go,' he clamped his knees tight, heaved hard on the reins to pull the horse around and raked the gelding's sides with his heels. It tossed its head, twisted as if to look back in disdain at this strange but strong, masterful rider, then leaped into a tight turn.

And through a sudden break in the high, drifting cloud, the moon bathed the grassland between creek and cottonwoods in a flood of pale white light.

A shot rang out.

The gelding shuddered. Its hind legs buckled. It was as if it had decided to sit down, propping itself up on stiff forelegs with head held high. Then, with a shuddering sigh, it toppled sideways and died. With his feet in stirrups, Gallant might have struggled to get free and been trapped beneath the horse's weight. As it was, he was able without thought to throw himself clear. The gelding fell on its left side. Gallant had kept a tight hold on the saddle horn. Now, moving fast, he pulled himself up, leaned across the horse's bulk and dragged Danson's 1860 lever-action Henry from its saddle boot. Another shot rang out. The bullet hissed overhead. Gallant flopped back on to the grass.

For the second time in the short space of fifteen minutes he was pinned down behind a warm, dead body. But this time, he was in real trouble. His flat-crowned black hat was between his shoulder blades, held by the leather neck strap. The moon was still in clear sky, and Gallant knew his thick mane of hair, light straw in colour, would be shining like a beacon. It had drawn that second shot.

That, Gallant thought wryly, was the good news. The bad news was that, over the crackling camp-fire, Danson had told the story as he'd seen it, but the conclusions he had drawn when up that steep track opposite the Last Chance saloon had been wrong. Horses wander as they graze. Seeing one on a rough patch of scrub in Salvation Creek didn't mean there wasn't another one there, hidden by the house – any more than it needed two men to answer the door when barman Jake Arkle made a surprise call. So it was a case not of one man remaining behind while his colleague, Quint, chased after Gord Eagan, but of two remaining in Salvation Creek to see if Born Gallant surfaced, and if he did, to follow him to hell and back.

The shot that killed Danson's black gelding, the one that whistled over Gallant's blond thatch, had not been fired by the man in the cottonwoods: those bullets had been fired by a rifleman somewhere out on the open prairie on the far side of the creek. Quint and Largo, place them where you will, the odds against were now two to one. Frequently faced by Gallant over the years, and always overcome, but never from a position of such disadvantage. He was pinned down, in bright moonlight, caught in a cross-fire and with only his two legs to carry him to safety.

SIX

A tense silence settled over the moonlit expanse of open grass between creek and cottonwoods. The rattle of gunfire had quietened birds and beasts, sent them winging to roost in their nests, soft-padding to curl up in their lairs. It was the heavy, stifling calm that precedes an inevitable storm, but inevitable didn't mean imminent. On the contrary, Gallant sensed that the two men chasing him had got this far, then run out of ideas.

Always willing to be scrupulously fair and look at a difficult situation from both sides, he could under-stand their dilemma. Trailing two men from Salvation Creek had been easy, too damn easy, and the well-worked ambush from the cottonwoods had ended with one of those men dead and Gallant pinned down. Danson's black gelding was also dead, and by now Gallant's roan could be half a mile away. If he did manage to break out of the trap, he'd be on foot and running for his life.

For Quint and Largo then, so far, so good.

But that was only half of a tough job. Pinned down he might be, but Gallant was heavily armed and now able to return fire from behind the solid, meaty bulk of a dead horse. He'd be exposed if they used out-flanking tactics, but the creek on one side and cottonwoods on the other made that manoeuvre difficult. So while his position remained perilous there was now impasse, a deadlock, a Mexican stand off – or something with an entirely different name in another ancient language, Gallant thought, grinning, because it was a not unfamiliar situation for a man who had resisted fierce attacks by bearded Pathan tribesmen skilled with sharp knives and their long-barrelled Jezails.

He did now what had helped him survive those tense struggles in the fierce heat of the Indian sub-continent. He made himself comfortable. First, he placed his flat-crowned black hat on his head and tightened the thong under his chin. Blond hair hidden. Beacon extinguished. Then he topped up the ammunition for Danson's Henry repeater by filling his pockets with cartridges from cartons found in the saddle-bag on the gelding's upper flank. From that same saddle-bag – being careful to keep his head down – he took the big man's water canteen and drank deeply. And through all of this important and mildly therapeutic activity Gallant's mind was working hard on the problem of what he could do to stay alive.

The moonlight faded, then went out. It was as if a

lamp-glass had been raised in an already gloomy room and someone had blown out the flame.

The fade was not instant, but fast enough to set Gallant's pulse racing as the break in the clouds closed and the shadow raced across the prairie, bringing almost total darkness.

My sainted uncle, Gallant thought, that's twice in a single skirmish and both times in my favour.

Then, as if a rodeo starting gun had fired, he was on the move, thrusting hard against the dead gelding to gain his feet. Breaking into a crouching run, Henry repeater held low, voicing silent thanks to his subconscious for the cruel move that had dumped Danson's body on the flames, to the gusting wind for the accommodating cloud cover that provided the second blackout. He ran with speed, with a clear aim in mind, and the direction he took was chosen because it was the shortest distance between two points. Not back to the blackened embers of the fire where Danson lay dead, which would have taken him into the closing jaws of that deadly crossfire. Not in a desperate sprint in the opposite direction, which *might* have taken him all the way to his skittish, wandering roan but was more likely to have seen him down on the ground and dying with a bullet or two in the back.

He ran for the thick stand of cottonwoods.

Damn me, he thought, wrong tactics, don't you know, cos I'm carrying a rifle, and handling a rifle in thick timber is like playing baseball underwater. But. . . .

He reached the fringe of the trees, breathless, kept his balance with a hand thrust against a rough tree trunk, then crashed into the thick undergrowth; thanked the Lord that his silent sprint across the wet grass hadn't drawn a single shot from Largo – or Quint – out in the open on the far side of the creek but as good as blind. Gasping, Gallant steadied himself for a second or two then ploughed on. It was a stumbling run through woods fully fifty yards deep, a desperate tearing run through clawing branches and with undergrowth snagging his boots. A fight to stay on his feet and keep moving – keep a grip on that damned rifle – that saw him finally break clear of the woods but kicked up enough noise to raise the dead.

But what worried Gallant wasn't the dead Danson and his poor, lifeless gelding.

The man who had planted a bullet in Danson's head was in the woods, but on the side closer to the creek. The clear light of the moon had gone. He would be hoping that Gallant was still pinned down behind the dead gelding, but would be relying on his ears for information. So now he would be listening, and listening hard – and Gallant had instant proof that there was nothing wrong with his hearing.

'Largo!' the outlaw yelled. 'Largo, he's on the move, get over here now.'

That informed Gallant that it was Largo in the open across the creek, Quint in the woods; but that fact had no sooner sunk home – for what it was worth – and Quint's desperate yell faded into silence, when there was more fierce crackling of branches and undergrowth. Quint had left his position and begun fighting his way through the cottonwoods. But Gallant knew that he again had the advantage. Quint's yell told of his fear that Gallant was getting away. He would be throwing caution to the winds, and out in the open, Gallant could hear his every move, his every curse.

The cards were falling in Gallant's favour, and that winning streak continued: on a night when gusts of wind were moving high clouds erratically, light began returning. This time there was no break in the clouds, but a definite thinning. Stygian darkness became faint moonlight akin to the eerie light that precedes every dawn. Gallant could hear Quint, and he was now aided by sight – the tossing of branches, as of a fox running through a field of tall corn, gave away the gunman's position. Halfway through the woods. Then three-quarters, and revealing more with every fighting lunge as the overhead leaf cover thinned and let through the light. A dark shape. A big man with a body wider than any cottonwood's trunk. A target a former British Army marksman could not miss.

Gallant cocked the Henry repeater, tucked the rifle into his shoulder and fired once, twice, three times.

Deep in the woods, crouched over the body of the man called Quint, Gallant gazed dispassionately at the outlaw's blood-soaked shirt and listened to the thud of hoofs followed by a wild splashing and the harder clatter of iron shoes on stone. Largo was answering the call for help at full speed.

'A bit bally late for your friend, don't you know,' Gallant whispered, and he gave Quint's pale dead cheek a consoling pat. More of a slap, actually, because he was in no mood for niceties and this man had killed, and would have killed again. Largo, bless him, was crossing the creek in answer to a desperate cry for help, but heading for a whole lot of grief. With a grim set to his face Gallant worked his way through trees and thorny thickets to meet the threat, at times using the Henry's barrel to slash furiously at branches that had whipped back to lash his face.

He reached the edge of the woods. Held back under cover. Listened. Heard more splashing, then a scrambling, the tearing of sod, the fall of stones from a riverbank – then the sudden thud of a horse's hoofs, now on soft earth with a covering of grass.

Heading away south, in one hell of a hurry.

Gallant, puzzled, used the Henry to create a space in a thick bush and gingerly poked his head out. The moonlight was about as helpful as a single candle in a vast subterranean mausoleum, the dark bulk of the racing horse almost lost against the background of even darker trees.

It was a good two hundred yards away, and going like the wind.

Largo, Gallant thought, heard three shots from a single rifle with no response, put two and two together, tacked my reputation on the end of the equation and decided being a live coward made excellent sense. No doubt he'd tell the Eagans some tale concocted on his lonely ride south, raise his own contribution in the gunfight to something heroic, and express deep but false regret at being unable to save poor Quint.

Relaxed, his mind easier, now thinking ahead to El Dorado and the captive Melody Lake and wondering how far his roan had strayed, Gallant stepped out of the woods. There he stopped. For some reason instinct caused him to glance towards the creek. Then he shook his head. There was no movement. Largo had hightailed, the craven outlaw was heading for the hills. Gallant stretched, held the rifle high and wide with hands at the ends of barrel and butt. He stretched his arms luxuriously outwards, easing the tenseness from stiff shoulder muscles.

Then, out in the open, totally exposed – posed like a bally fool reaching for the stars, he was to think later – realization kicked in and he knew he'd slipped up badly.

He'd seen the shape of a racing horse, but not the shape of its rider. And in the act of easing shoulder muscles he'd felt a shape that should not have been there. Whipping branches that had raised painful wheals on his face had torn his black hat from his head. It hung between his shoulder blades, the soft pressure telling him that his blond hair was again catching the light. In that fraction of a second's realization he knew he'd walked into a clever trap. Largo had slipped from the saddle and sent his horse running free. In that same fraction of a second, in that blink of an eye that saw Gallant snatch down the rifle and drop to one knee as he began to turn, he heard the musical tinkle of spurs away to his left. Then Largo's rifle spat its deadly chunk of hot lead.

It was like being gored in the shoulder by a charging longhorn steer. The sheer weight of the shot from a powerful rifle spun Gallant bodily round and dumped him on the earth. He fell on his left side, bloody shoulder hard against the ground. That put his right side uppermost. In the fall his right hand had been flung behind him, outstretched. The extreme end of the Henry repeater's barrel was clutched in his iron grip. A dead man's grip, Gallant thought, and snapped his jaw shut in fury, breath whistling through flared nostrils.

Pain was liquid fire, agony washing like molten lava across Gallant's chest. Sickness welled, in his stomach, in his throat. He felt his senses slipping away. Through a shimmering blur, through the dizzy sense of spinning into the final abyss, he again heard the tinkle of spur rowels. Envisaged the tall man, moving closer, one careful step at a time. Rifle cocked, aim steady on the fallen man.

The fallen man gritted his teeth and thought, keep coming at your peril, my friend, there are more ways than one to skin a cat. He banished pain from his mind; forced himself to stay still; to play dead now – or end up dead. Through eyelids that he opened to the merest of slits he caught a glimpse of Largo, the man he had first seen playing poker in the Last

Chance saloon, had last seen up against the saloon's wall under Frank Lake's gun. A tall, lean shape outlined against the night skies. Three paces away. Then, a single, jingling step. Now two short paces away – and the rifle was lifted. Settled. Its aim downwards

In one smooth movement Gallant rolled on to his face, brought the Henry rifle whipping over at the full extent of his right arm. Largo saw it coming. His finger closed on the rifle's trigger. Muzzle-flame flared red, the shot cracked. But the surprised outlaw had jerked back and the bullet drilled inches wide. Gallant heard it thud into the earth by his hip.

Then the Henry's butt smashed against the side of Largo's head.

SEVEN

Still rocky on his feet, pain knifing through his shoulder with every throbbing beat of his pulse, Gallant left the unconscious outlaw and walked away from the trees. It was autumn, now long past midnight and very cold. The high cloud had further thinned, the moon was a weak glimmer but in evidence nonetheless. In its wan light a mist could be seen settling over the creek and spreading out to either side, dampening the grass. There was the smell of rushing creek water, of fallen yellow leaves curled and decaying in the tangled woods.

Gallant gazed towards the south, put two fingers to his lips and gave a shrill whistle. In that eerie setting it was a mournful sound, the cry of a bird keening for a lost soul mate, of a warrior close to death after a battle long past, but it got its reward. Out of the mist came trotting not one horse, but two, and Gallant looked on that as proof of the turnaround in his fortunes that had come when the Henry's butt almost removed Largo's head from his shoulders.

He welcomed the roan with a gentling hand on its neck – necessary because the big horse had instantly picked up the scent of fresh blood. That same coppery smell saw Largo's horse – another black gelding – walk close to the downed man, then back off a short way, nostrils flared.

Awkwardly unbuckling his saddlebag flap with his good hand, Gallant found the pack of wound dressings. He led the roan to the shelter of the trees where the bite of the cold was less, then slipped his shirt from his shoulder and assessed what he could do to tend to his wound. It was far less serious than he'd expected; as soon as he regained his feet he'd realized that the bullet had ripped on through. The blow had been a solid one, and perhaps the hot lead had chipped bone – time would tell – and as for infection, well. . .

Dipping again into the saddle-bag, Gallant located the small bottle of Tennessee whiskey he always carried with him, and unscrewed the cap. He hesitated, clamped his eyes shut and poured a generous splash of the raw spirit on to the wound. His cry was an involuntary yelp of pain as the strong whiskey bit into the open, bloody flesh. As quick as a flash he threw his head back, poured an equal measure of whiskey into his mouth and swallowed the lot in one gulp. A full minute later he was still gasping, choking, eyes streaming, but well on the way to being suitably numbed.

'Kill or cure, gunshot wounds, snakebite or the dreaded lurgy,' he said, grinning at the watching horses as he slipped the half-empty bottle into his waistcoat pocket. Then, breathing less ragged, he finished tending to his wound and buttoned his shirt.

And then there was Largo. Flat on his back. Unmoving.

Gallant crouched by the outlaw. He reached across, picked up the Winchester rifle that had sent a bullet through his shoulder and tossed it into the woods. The man's six-gun he plucked from its holster and flung backhand in the general direction of the creek. He leaned forward, located a pulse in the man's neck; dropped to one knee as Largo sensed the touch and groaned. His eyes flickered open. Gallant watched with interest as full consciousness returned, and with it Largo's swift recollection of how he had been viciously clubbed, the acute awareness that he was now at Gallant's mercy. The outlaw's body tensed. A hand came up, gingerly touched the bloody swelling above his ear.

'Welcome back,' Gallant said. 'Care for a drink, old boy?'

'You're a dead man,' Largo said hoarsely.

'Well, actually, just the opposite, and in your position I'd be inclined not to push my luck. The offer of a drink still stands, by the way, despite your infernal cheek.'

He stood, grabbed a handful of the outlaw's shirt and dragged him bodily to his feet. Propped the unsteady man against a tree trunk. Handed him the whiskey bottle, then stepped back and drew his Peacemaker.

'Finish that,' Gallant said, 'then there's things I need you to do.'

'What *I* need to do,' Largo said, drinking, then pursing his lips and sending a jet of whiskey in the direction of Gallant's boots, 'is finish you. And I'll do that. . .'

'Unsaddle your horse. Take off that split-ear head-stall, the curb bit. Fashion some kind of a hackamore from that rope you've got looped from your saddle. When that's done, take off your boots, your socks. . .

'In a pig's. . .

'Do it now, all of it, or I'll put a bullet in your knee.' And Gallant noisily cocked the Peacemaker.

For a long thirty seconds of tense silence, their gazes locked. Then Largo swore under his breath and walked over to his horse. Working angrily, pain tilting his head to one side, he undid the cinch, removed the saddle. Held it, looked at Gallant.

'In the woods.'

Again the muttered curse. A moment's pause. A glance at the shiny Peacemaker and a shake of the head. He hefted the saddle over to the trees, caught the gleam of his rifle in the undergrowth. He dropped the saddle on the rifle, bent to retrieve his rope. Back at the horse he removed the rest of the rig, flipped open his pocket knife to cut a section of rope and fashion and fix in place a crude hack-amore. Then he stepped back, looked at Gallant.

'Boots, socks,' Gallant said.

Largo scowled. He was a swarthy man, unshaven. His hat had gone, knocked clean off his head by the mighty blow from Gallant's rifle; his hair was unkempt and bloody. His belt was loaded with shells, but he had no six-gun. The threat of a smashed kneecap or two was forcing him to follow Gallant's orders. But his black eyes were gleaming in the faint moonlight, and Gallant was keenly aware that this man, who had most certainly been the brains behind the carefully laid trap, was still scheming.

And in the instant that that thought crossed his mind, Largo acted.

He drew back his arm as if to rub at the scalp wound. He used the hand holding the knife. The move was meant to fool Gallant, or at best catch him unawares for the fractions of a second needed. It did that. Gallant saw the move. Yelled a fierce, 'No, Largo.' Began raising his Peacemaker, tightening his finger on the trigger. But Largo's hand was already snapping forward. Cold steel flashed in the moon-light. The thrown knife spun wickedly towards Gallant. Instinctively, he ducked away. At the same moment, Largo dropped to a crouch. Then he charged.

The knife's blade sliced the tip of Gallant's ear. He felt the sudden sharp pain. Then the lean outlaw's shoulder slammed into his middle. Driven by the outlaw's full weight Gallant went over backwards, almost blacked out at the agony of his wounded shoulder hitting the ground. That pain took away what was left of his breath. He could not suck air into his lungs because he found it impossible to breathe. He knew from experience that a fierce blow to the

70

solar plexus paralyses a man's diaphragm. And Largo had planned well: it's almost impossible for a man to defend himself against a surprise, double attack.

Largo was quite literally pressing home his advantage. He flattened himself, spread his weight, easily holding Gallant down. His bony, muscular forearm he used like an iron bar, ramming it in under Gallant's chin. Choking, twisting, writhing, Gallant was staring wildly at a high moon turning blood red as he ran out of oxygen and his eyes filmed. Largo simply lay still, his full weight on his forearm. His head was on one side, resting on Gallant's chest.

And Gallant, one arm flung wide, fist clenched, still held his Peacemaker.

With the last of his strength, he lifted that arm, held it high, then brought the six-gun down and delivered a desperate, last chance blow to Largo's skull, his wounded scalp. Blood splashed, hot on Gallant's face. Beneath the crack of metal on bone he thought he heard a faint moan. Suddenly there was a subtle, indefinable change in the weight holding him down; the man lying across Gallant was now unconscious, or dead.

'And I, don't you know,' Gallant croaked into the unresponsive outlaw's ear, 'am turning into a predictable bally so-and-so renowned only for hitting men on the head with heavy bits of metal.'

There was no more resistance. Gallant wriggled out from under Largo's weight, used the outlaw's Stetson to fetch water from the creek and pour it over his head. He stood back, watched impassively as Largo spluttered, coughed, rolled on to his back and blinked up at the sky. Then Gallant dropped to his knees, wrenched off both the man's stovepipe boots and filthy socks and hurled the lot towards the creek.

For the second time he grabbed fistfuls of the man's shirt and pulled him to his feet. He spun the groggy outlaw bodily, pushed him hard and sent him staggering towards his horse.

'Climb aboard,' Gallant said, 'point him north and head back the way you came. No doubt sooner or later you'll recover and start dreaming about vengeance. You do that, the dream will turn into a nightmare. Forget the Eagans, forget you ever heard of Melody Lake. If I catch sight of you in El Dorado, I will kill you.'

EIGHT

At midday, two days later, Born Gallant rode into El Dorado. He was dusty, tired from the long ride, and had been looking forward with keen anticipation to a first night in a feather bed: goodbye to Danson's stable, and cold nights under the stars. At first sight of the town, that now seemed like a forlorn hope. Always had been, he supposed; this wasn't England, where the mansion on the sprawling family estate was serviced by ladies' maids, housemaids, laundry maids, kitchen maids and scullery maids up to their elbows in washing-up water.

Not to mention the cook, Gallant thought, his stomach rumbling.

He'd told Frank Lake that he'd once ridden through El Dorado on his way to Dodge City, but in truth he had no recollection of that previous visit. Perhaps, he thought, ruefully eyeing the settlement, that was because he had blinked. The impression now was of a meagre scattering of dwellings and business premises along the banks of the Walnut River, the town's population likely to be in the low hundreds. On his short and fatal ride from Salvation Creek, Karl Danson had told Gallant that El Dorado dated from 1870. It could be reached, he'd said, from the Flint Hills town of Florence by a branch line built by the Walnut Valley Railroad Company.

Its name, Danson had added with that wide, bearded grin, was of Spanish origin and meant 'golden land'.

Gallant wasn't misled, or impressed: this was a shabby new town with little chance of reaching a respectable old age.

His deceptively leisurely but far from lazy approach was along a rough pathway close to the river. Slouched in the saddle, he was keenly observing everything and everybody that moved. He was, he warned himself, now in the town named by Frank Lake as being close to where his granddaughter was being held. Mention had been made of the Flint Hills, and a possible outlaw hideout – but that was pure speculation.

As for movement, well, midday was the time most working folk relaxed. In front of him on the riverbank a dog was sprawled in a patch of grass, scratching itself with a hind leg. A few women wearing hats, long gingham frocks and high-laced boots were chatting outside the general store where goods were displayed in wire racks. A man in a black suit was emerging from the open door of a gun-

74

smith's carrying two rifles in the crook of his arm and saying something over his shoulder – and, suddenly, he stopped.

Some sound or movement had attracted his attention, and he had turned to look further up what passed for the El Dorado main street – most of the buildings faced the river, so the street was a one-sided wide expanse of dirt that in a more prosperous town might have been called the square. The dark-suited man's gaze seemed, to Gallant, to be fixed on the building that had SALOON painted in crude black lettering high on the false front.

As Gallant gave the roan its head and was taken at walking pace away from the river and closer to the uneven line of the buildings, he saw that two men had walked out of the saloon on to the rough plank walk. The whip-thin man leading the way was hatless, the holster hanging from his gunbelt flapping as he walked because it was weightless, empty of any weapon. Behind him, the badge on the burly moustachioed man's vest glittered in the winter sunshine, a gleam matched by the bright shine on the six-gun he held down by his thigh. Not pointing. Not threatening. But ready for any and every eventuality, and a warning to the man in front not to turn and fight, or break and run.

Still on the plank walk, keeping to the shade, they passed close to Gallant. Booted feet thudded. Old, warped timber creaked underfoot. The man in front flashed a quick look at Gallant, then away. The second man's gaze was more direct and penetrating, revealing the usual small town marshal's suspicion of every gun-toting newcomer.

Gallant returned the lawman's curt nod, then pulled the roan in close to the plank walk and turned it so that he could watch the two men. Fifty yards away he now noticed another sign, one he'd missed on his way in. This one said JAIL, and it was on a board nailed to the town's only building built of stone.

Well, of course, Gallant thought with a grim smile, where else would a town marshal be taking his prisoner? He touched his horse with his heels, let it carry him after the two men but kept well back. The marshal, without the benefit of having eyes in the back of his head, would nevertheless be aware of his movements. Gallant did not want to appear threatening.

Ten minutes into the town – and it had started. In a way that was so totally unexpected he would be forced to play the cards as they fell. Which was in no way a disadvantage. Somewhere, at some time, he'd been told that when on to a good thing, a man should stick with it.

So Gallant would play the same old hand that almost always saw him with a fair chance of raking in the pot. When he tied up at the hitch rail in front of the single-storey stone building and followed the two men inside, he intended to be once again the harmless blond-haired English fool, anxiously stuttering as he enquired as to what his friend might have done, for goodness sake, to warrant arrest at gunpoint.

76

For the lean man with the empty holster who had flashed that one, carefully guarded glance at Gallant was no stranger, but the journalist, Stick McCrae.

NINE

'That was easier than expected. Fastest and most peaceful jail break on record occurred today in the town of El Dorado. Our man on the spot tells the story.'

'Very funny,' McCrae said. 'My arrest was as genuine as a wooden Indian outside a big city dime store. Winfield is a lawman balanced on a shaky fence. Watched closely by the richest rancher in this part of Kansas – who helps pay his wages – he's careful to show adherence to rules but also his utter disdain for the man's attempts at control.'

'So in the establishment where we now sit drinking what tastes like moonshine whiskey, you dumped said rancher's straw boss in the sawdust with a swift sock to the jaw, accidentally trod on his face – twice, so I've been informed – and Winfield took you in for violent affray but it was all show?'

'The strawboss is Dean Kenny. And the stamping was no accident.'

Gallant raised an eyebrow. 'Stamping? Then no,

no accident, and somewhere around our second drink – if we escape fatal poisoning from the first – you'll be telling me the motive behind that uncharacteristic aggression.'

'Uncharacteristic? Are you serious?'

'I retract uncharacteristic. But, talking of genuine, Marshal Winfield's appreciation of my sparkling performance in his office seemed a little forced.'

'He'd been warned, which is the only reason he didn't fall over laughing,' Stick McCrae said. 'I introduced myself as soon as I rode into town, told him about my piece in the *Dodge Times*.'

'Which was all about Melody Lake and would see me galloping south on my trusty steed to save the damsel in distress,' Gallant said, grinning. 'Would it surprise you to know I didn't read it?'

'No. Why should a blue blood soil his hands on a Dodge City rag? But in that case, what brought you to El Dorado?'

'It's a long story.'

The telling was swift, and Gallant's tumble into the cold waters of Salvation Creek, the crack on his head, had McCrae suppressing laughter. But mention of Karl Danson and his killing by the gunslinger Quint brought a swift change. He frowned, and his eyes narrowed.

'Did you know there were two Dansons?' McCrae said.

'Really? Well, after that cold water dunking it was Karl who dressed my wounds, and volunteered to help me in the search for Melody.'

'That crack on the head addled your brain. Danson wasn't helping you, you were helping him. Some time last year the Eagans shot Karl's brother stone cold dead over a poker game in Abilene. Karl was using you to lead him to his brother's killers – and you still haven't told me why you're here.'

'You heard of Frank Lake?'

'Melody's grandfather.'

'That's right. At risk of complicating an already twisted tale, we were both in Salvation Creek because of separate visits to the Pinkerton's Kansas City office. Lake came over to me at the bar in the Last Chance, asked me to find his granddaughter and bring her home.'

McCrae's grin and shake of the head expressed utter astonishment.

'Now, this time you must be joking.'

'Why?'

'Chet and Gord Eagan may be the muscle behind Melody's kidnapping, but you must know they were under orders. The man giving the orders would have been Emerson Judd, pretender to a minor throne, or one of his underlings. But what followed doesn't make any kind of sense. Which means, in my opinion, somewhere down the line of responsibility those orders were modified. My train of thought leads to just one conclusion.'

Gallant met McCrae's sardonic gaze. His mind was racing, and suddenly he was hit by his own stupidity, his blind gullibility. Orders modified? Softened? Well, yes, of course they were. He grimaced, looked into his empty glass, then swore softly and slammed it on the table.

'On the ride south there was a question tossed back and forth over the camp fire,' he said. 'And neither Danson nor I could come up with an answer. It was this: why was the feisty lawyer Melody Lake taken in a Kansas City street, dragged all the way to El Dorado and kept under guard, when a bullet in the head would have solved all Emerson Judd's problems?'

'That would almost certainly have been his original order,' McCrae agreed. 'It didn't happen, Judd changed his mind. He must have been under intense pressure – but from whom?'

'From whom?' Gallant echoed, grinning. 'Well, the *whom* we're looking for has to be her grandfather, doesn't it? Frank Lake. He's the man most likely to have Melody's best interests at heart. He got wind of Judd's plans for her, was forced to go along with 'em but got the plan changed from killing to kidnapping and what we in England would call transportation: young girls sent to the colonies for stealing a loaf of bread, that sort of thing. Lake got his granddaughter's death sentence commuted to confinement in a cosy cell in downtown El Dorado.'

'Bit of wishful thinking there, but yes, my conclusions exactly,' McCrae said. 'Lake was the one putting on pressure, but this is where we come to the bit about none of it making any sense.'

'Which it doesn't. If we're right, Melody is here because of her grandpappy – but why the hell has he sent me chasing down here to pluck her from the clutches of the same men who have, in essence, been agreeing to his terms?'

TEN

They emerged from the saloon early in the afternoon, crossed the street to El Dorado's only café. It was a single-storey shack next door to the livery barn, outside which the town's windmill creaked wearily in the light breeze. Water dribbled into the communal horse trough, where a lean ranch hand was holding his cow pony's reins as it dipped its head to drink.

As they ate surprisingly good steak, eggs and potatoes, the ripe ambience amused Gallant. The sweating, aproned cook had wiped his glistening brow, then opened both the café's front windows to let out the smoke and greasy fumes from an iron stove that glowed cherry red. But he'd succeeded only in letting in the rich smell of straw and horses, which ripened as it warmed.

'Compared to that,' Gallant said, sniffing appreciatively, 'the hottest of English mustards is as nothing.'

'Yeah, well, that's as maybe, but one thing you said puzzled me, led me to do some thinking,' McCrae said, as he pushed away his empty plate and wiped his mouth on his bandanna. 'It's this: you said grand-pappy Lake has Melody's best interests at heart. But the plan he got changed to save her life still hogties the young lady lawyer. With the only willing lawyer in chains, Judd is still on track for high office in Washington.'

'Contradictions whichever way you look at it,' Gallant said, eyes thoughtful as he watched the cowboy mount, and ride away. 'Frank Lake must be backing Emerson Judd – God knows why – but he draws the line at seeing his granddaughter harmed. He arranges for her to be kept safe, but a long way from that courtroom. Straightforward so far: Lake's a tender-hearted family man, but for some damned reason he's rooting for a corrupt politician. But then we ask ourselves that question: why? What's Judd done for Lake to gain his support?'

'Done *to* Lake,' McCrae said, rolling a cigarette. 'He's threatened him.'

'In what way? And why has Lake now changed his mind, decided that he can no longer support Judd? Which he must have done. If we snatch Melody from the Eagans' clutches and get her back to Kansas City, she'll trot into that courtroom with her dark hair flying, carrying a smart leather briefcase stuffed with incriminating documents. Judd's ambitions will be in shreds, and who's he going to blame?'

'Frank Lake.'

Gallant shook his head. 'The Lakes, plural.'

McCrae was relaxed in his chair. His back was to

84

the windows.

'That straw boss you socked, Kenny,' Gallant said. 'He's tall, lean, dark hair a mite grey at the temples?'

'And a swelling to the jaw,' McCrae added, grinning. 'He may also be favouring one leg, because he went down hard.'

'I watched him water his horse. He's ridden out of town. Unless he's blind, he'll have seen me follow you and Winfield into the jail. He'll surely have recognized me from a description.'

'Recognized you, and received a warning. There's a railroad, and railroad means telegraph. Kenny's boss likes to keep in touch with Kansas City. I think his strawboss calls in the telegraph office most days to pick up any news.'

'And today that news was bad,' Gallant said. 'He's heading back to the ranch.'

'Which is what we do next, or as near as we can get,' McCrae said. 'I want to show you the property owned by Kenny's boss.'

'Who – let me guess – is a rich man backing Judd.'

'And not just with money. His property stretches all the way to the Flint Hills. Shallow canyons. Lots of timber – and a number of line cabins, empty most of the time.'

'But right now not all of those cabins are empty,' Gallant said, watching McCrae.

The journalist nodded. 'That's the way I see it. One of them will recently have been put to good use.'

'Nothing much more to be said,' Gallant said,

'other than to ask you if this rancher has a name?'

'Sure he has,' McCrae said, sliding back his chair. 'His name is Mason Judd. He's Emerson Judd's elder brother.'

ELEVEN

A man was coming out of Emerson Judd's office when his wife arrived. He was fat, bearded, his remaining hair like lines scrawled across his skull by a fine twig dipped in lamp black. Leonora Judd gasped as the stench of stale beer and cigars hit her as he approached, then threatened to pull her in his wake the way an ebb tide sucks at a pebbled beach. He thumped down the stairs. She entered the office, slammed the door and leaned back against the solid oak.

'Who the hell was that?'

'A man bearing bad news.'

'From?'

'Salvation Creek.'

'Which tells me nothing. What's going on, Emerson?'

Judd was standing by the tall window behind his desk, looking out over Kansas City. It was a fine vista, but today it left him unmoved. His imagination, for

87

several years, had him in a much finer office affording a far grander view over Washington. That situation had, tantalisingly, been drawing ever closer. Today the news brought to him by the Last Chance barkeep, Jake Arkle, warned Judd that he had been wrong to allow a moment of weakness to seriously warp his judgement.

'Grab yourself a drink,' he said and, away from the window and now standing in front of his desk, he watched his tall, blonde wife – sure to draw all eyes when he took her to the nation's capital city – pour dry sherry from a crystal decanter into a crystal glass and turn to stare at him with a cynical smile and eyes sharp enough to make all that fine glassware's cut facets appear dull.

'Salvation Creek,' Leonora said. 'A one horse town. No, not even that, maybe just one lame mule. Home to a couple of gun-slinging range drifters used by the Eagans. So if that smelly nobody was the bearing of tidings other than glad, they must be about those two and a certain young lady lawyer who has conveniently gone missing.'

'According to Arkle. . .

'Arkle?'

'Barkeep at the Last Chance saloon. Maybe the owner.' Judd shrugged. 'Smelly he may be, but like every man behind every saloon bar in the land, he keeps his eyes and ears open. He witnessed a late-night incident, a conversation between two men. When he reported what he'd heard to Quint and Largo – the two drifters – they saddled up and headed south.'

'In pursuit of. . . ?'

'Born Gallant.'

'If the Creek's a one mule town,' Leonora said, 'that Englishman is a five-minute wonder hardly worth a couple of lines of news print. A spent force. Shot his bolt.'

'And if you were writing my speeches, they'd be riddled with clichés.' Judd shook his head. 'I'm not sure I agree. But it doesn't matter. He's riding to El Dorado to snatch Melody Lake, but the Eagans put a lot of trust in Quint and Largo. If they're on his tail, Gallant's a dead man.'

'So what's the concern? A minor problem, halfway to being solved.'

'Oh, don't worry, the young lady's going nowhere. But according to Arkle, Gallant rode south at the request of the man who persuaded me to change my mind about putting that damned interfering lawyer into permanent retirement.'

'Old Frank Lake? That can't be right.'

Judd nodded. 'I had him over a barrel because he knows that if my political opponent becomes senator he'll land grab to draw settlers into the area. Lake's ranch, several thousand acres standing idle since his retirement, will be among the first to be taken. The seriousness of the situation was passed to him in detail by his son. . .

'Now dead.'

'Yes. Father took his late son's advice. Had to: he had no option but to support me – or at the very least, not disrupt my campaign. And he reluctantly agreed to his granddaughter being taken out of the picture, provided I guaranteed that she would come to no harm.'

'So how has your hold on him been weakened?'

'Unlike his predecessor, the new Pinkerton man, Grant, isn't fond of politicians, isn't open to . . . persuasion. Lake got him to look into his son's death. See who was behind his killing.'

For a brief moment there was a stunned silence. Then Leonora exploded.

'You stupid, stupid bastard.'

'Wha. . .

'If Frank has now gone against you, despite the possibility that he'll lose his property and his home, then that can mean but one thing. For some damn crazy reason you got a hired gun to . . . to. . .

Rendered speechless, her eyes were blazing. She moved towards her husband, the empty glass in her hand gripped tight enough to whiten her knuckles. Judd was also moving. They met in the centre of the room. Before she could strike – the intent clear in her bright blue eyes – Judd put his hand on her shoulder to hold her still then drew back his arm and slapped her across the face.

It was done with force. The blow snapped her head around. On her face the imprint of his palm was white, then flooded with red. The muscle he'd put into the slap caused her to take a sideways step. Her shoe caught in the thick carpet fronting the desk. She almost went down. Almost. Not quite. And when she'd regained her poise – despite the thin trickle of blood on her upper lip – in some uncanny way she read her husband's mind, and she was smirking as she put his previous thoughts into words.

'In your dealings with Frank Lake you let a moment of weakness seriously warp your judgement. It could finish you. With you down, then I'm out of here.'

'I'm allowed that one moment, but you can rest assured that I learn from even the smallest of mistakes. Frank Lake will pay. His granddaughter's safety is no longer guaranteed – by now the Eagans will have got their new orders – and the next time old man Lake walks out his front door he'll be cut in two by the blast from a double-barrelled shotgun.'

TWELVE

The sun was on its long slow drift down to hills that were gold-painted smudges in the far distant west. Despite the onset of winter, it had spent the long day warming the land. Five miles north of El Dorado, Gallant and McCrae were away from their horses, hats tipped down over their eyes, gazing west. They were standing on the edge of a grove of pines on a ridge perhaps a hundred feet high, which was about as high as you could get on the Kansas prairies. The late afternoon light was in their faces. In front of them the land sloped gradually, rough grass dotted with clumps of chaparral, until after a hundred yards or so it levelled.

Another half mile, and two huge timber gateposts set either side of a wide dirt track that had its beginnings in El Dorado marked the entrance to the Mason Judd property. A flat board joined the posts some eight feet above the track. A little way off the board's centre, fixed by carpenter's nails, there hung a longhorn steer's yellowing skull. Then the name, perfectly centred, black lettering seared into the wood with a red-hot branding iron. Nothing fancy. Just the one word: Judd. Which could have been the mark of a modest man, eschewing a fancy name for the property, but was far more likely to be an indication of supreme arrogance.

The placement of the skull, Gallant surmised, might have been intended as a grim warning. Keep away. It seemed to be working. The low ranch house, yard, barns and corrals – another half mile away – showed no signs of life, either two- or four-legged.

'Judd's a rancher,' Gallant said, gazing out over the property. 'Where are the cows?'

'He sells beef, not milk,' McCrae said.

'There's nothing there to sell.'

'He's moved operations. Once he had longhorn herds on land to the north. Then he changed tack. Heard about George Grant, who in '73 brought four Angus bulls from Scotland to Victoria, right here in Kansas? So Judd went from quantity to quality. He imported Angus cattle of both sexes and began stocking the land away to the west. That's in the Flint Hills, but even in that expanse of undulating country the elevation never gets above 1,500 feet.'

'OK, so those line cabins we were talking about are away to the north and no longer in use,' Gallant said. 'Use of the usual kind, that is.' Then, more sombre, allowing his thoughts to wander down dark pathways, he mused, 'I was in Karl Danson's barn for one night, thought of it as my bedroom. If we're right, Melody's been held for a while now. D'you think she's grown

93

fond of her lonely cabin?'

'If it was lonely, that young lady wouldn't be there, Gallant. She's being held in a prison, not a goddamn bedroom. The cabin's guarded, night and day.'

'Right ho, yes, I think that was the message I was trying to get across in my own eccentric way. Lonely being part of it, as in isolated. What I'm getting at is that the little shack's likely to be open to attack from all sides. And I'm guessing the sides and the rear will have timber cover, making a silent and unobserved approach possible by intrepid rescuers. But before we go charging off like Cardigan and his Light Brigade at Balaclava, let's recap. Get fixed in our minds what we know for sure, then try to work out what we're up against.'

'The Eagans, that's what we know, that's all we know, everything else is conjecture,' McCrae said bluntly. 'Chet brought Melody to El Dorado. If brother Gord believes you're floating face down in that creek, he'll have come hot foot to lend a hand.'

'My being dead or alive would make no difference, Gord would have come anyway. As for Chet, on a three-day ride south there'd be two overnight stops. He wouldn't have been able to hold Melody on his own, so count on another two men. That's four we're up against.'

McCrae chewed that over, looked torn by indecision.

Gallant grinned. 'OK, that's guesswork again. And here's some more of the same. After the fight with Quint and Largo, I dragged Karl Danson's body into the woods, covered it as best I could. But I made a mistake not finishing Largo. Something tells me that, bareback, bare of foot, he watched my every move in that fitful moonlight. When I left he'd've waited a while, then gathered together all his belongings I'd tossed hither and yon and headed south.'

'So that makes it five.'

'Which, if we made our move in the dead of night, wouldn't be too many to handle. But that's not the worst of it. Once Jake Arkle, the *Last Chance*'s barman, saw me alive and kicking, the fat was in the fire. It was Jake sicced Quint and Largo on to me. His next move would have been to head for Kansas City and tell Emerson Judd that Frank Lake had changed his tune. Too late for Gord Eagan to bring that news to Mason Judd, but when Emerson Judd got wind of what was happening he wouldn't have wasted any time. . .

For a while there was silence. McCrae wandered back to the horses, got the makings from the jacket he'd thrown over his saddle, came back rolling a cigarette on the move. The match flared. He drew deep on the cigarette, narrowed his eyes against the smoke. Gallant had been pacing. His flat black hat hung at his back. His fair hair was a golden cap in the evening sun. He touched the butt of his Peacemaker, shook his head irritably, ran his fingers through the thick shock of hair and came over to McCrae.

'We can forget Largo,' Gallant said flatly. 'I told Largo to ride north, stay clear of El Dorado. He was a beaten man, we've nothing to fear from him—'

'Even if he has chanced his arm and ridden south?'

'Right. But Jake Arkle, the barman I had down as a bearded, brainless nincompoop, will – as I've already pointed out – have opened the can of worms and put the fat in the fire.' Ignoring McCrae's slow grin he went on, 'Involved from the moment I spoke to Frank Lake in the *Last Chance*, Arkle *will* have ridden to Kansas City, and he *will* have spoken to Emerson Judd, his secretary, his dog – doesn't matter. With that done. . .

'The wires to El Dorado would have been hot,' McCrae said. 'Brother to brother. Urgent action needed. So I'm wondering if Judd's straw boss, Dean Kenny, did go to the telegraph office today?'

'If he did, we're already running out of time – could be out of it altogether. Kenny was watering his horse outside the café, and we know he left town before us. Mason Judd got the news – courtesy of Arkle, brother Emerson and the miracle of the telegraph – and he could already have sent word to the Eagans: "*Imprisonment's at an end, fellers. Put a bullet in her head*".'

'Yes, but Judd's a hands-on rancher, with valuable cattle. Talking around town, I got the impression he spends most of the daylight hours with his expensive beef herds, miles away to the west. The spread looks quiet. Without the boss there in the house to make the decision, there's no way Kenny would take it on himself. . .

McCrae broke off. A man had ridden out of one of

the barns and across the distant yard, fiercely spurred his horse and was now tearing down the track towards the big timber gateway. As they watched, he came through at a gallop, almost clipping one of the heavy posts with his shoulder so tight was his turn. Then, leaving behind a cloud of dust that drifted like gunsmoke across the flat grassland, he headed for town.

'Well, what do you know,' McCrae breathed. 'For just about the first time in my life, I'm glad I got something wrong. Kenny must have been on his way to the telegraph office when I dumped him on his backside in the saloon. My punch addled his brain, turned the strawboss into a sober drunk who headed home in a dream. Now he's woken up, and he's in one hell of a hurry to pick up any messages and get back before Judd rides in.'

'So now,' Gallant said, 'we can take it that Melody's still alive, in the pink, sound in wind and limb and so on, and we're in a good position to put paid to any ideas Judd may have of summary execution. We wait. We watch. And then when it begins to happen – hours of darkness, wouldn't you say? – we're the two men playing follow my leader. Because,' Gallant said, 'the only way we can locate that line cabin is by following the men Judd sends out to kill Melody.'

THIRTEEN

It was gone midnight when the sound of hoofbeats reached Gallant and McCrae. As darkness fell, the night had turned wet. There was no wind, but a fine cold rain was falling on the Kansas plains. Despite the low cloud cover suggesting there was little likelihood of the moon breaking through, there was enough faint ambient light for them to see two men riding out of the Judd property and turning their horses towards the north.

At the edge of the trees on the high ground McCrae, hunched in the saddle, bundled up in a thick plaid mackinaw with the collar up around his ears and his dripping Stetson pulled down low, was putting voice to Gallant's thoughts.

'Two's a surprise. Surely one man would be capable of delivering a short message?'

'Especially,' Gallant said, 'as it'll take just one of those guarding Melody to carry out Judd's orders. But, two men or half-a-dozen, it's all playing out the way we expected.'

'If we've got it right.'

'Oh, it's right enough. We have to believe that, because to think otherwise could be leaving Melody to her fate. So now we take it as read that those two men are riding north with a signed death warrant.'

'You know, I think the second man's Mason Judd,' McCrae said. He'd poked back the wet brim of his Stetson with one finger and had been gazing with almost fierce concentration down the slope. The two riders had passed below them, still some way away but as close as they were going to get. One man lean and hawk-like despite his thick coat – possibly Kenny – the other big, burly, even in the faint light an imposing figure of a man exuding authority, riding what to Gallant's experienced eye looked like a thoroughbred stallion.

'Now, wouldn't that be a fine thing,' Gallant said softly. 'The big man himself, going to witness the killing so his brother will be in no doubt. But, as we're going to be there to foil his evil plans' – this with a grin at McCrae – 'the man's going to be eating crow – isn't that what they say out here?'

'He'll eat crow if we can trail them to wherever the hell they're going without being spotted,' McCrae said. 'If we're right and his strawboss picked up the telegraphed warning, Judd will be expecting you to come out of the darkness, all guns blazing.'

Oh, the warning had come, Gallant mused, of that there could be little doubt. Kenny had come riding back from town at dusk. Shortly after that, Judd and a bunch of his men had ridden in from tending to the prime beef herds to the far west of his property. With the horses unsaddled, fed and watered and let loose in the corral, the men had retired to the bunkhouse. Judd was already in the big house, the front door shut behind him. Then Kenny had appeared, walked up to the house, and been briefly silhouetted against warm lamplight that flooded the gallery as the door was opened to his confident knock.

'Yes,' Gallant said, 'Judd will be expecting trouble, and that makes it a knotty problem. Get too close, keep 'em in sight, and we give the game away. Stay too far back and follow their muddy tracks and the first we'll know of any cabin is when we hear the shots ending Melody's young life.'

'What we need,' McCrae said, 'is a British soldier of fortune experienced in desert warfare to come up with a plan.'

'And that's going to be of use on a rainy night in Kansas? Well, OK, why not? There's only so many ways of fightin' a war, and I'd say what we need here is guerrilla tactics; the kind of worrisome, irritating skirmishing that helped this land cock a snook at King George number three. Hit and run's another way of puttin' it: we hit, they run.'

'When you start talking like a fool,' McCrae said, 'I know you're running out of ideas.'

'If following those fellers too close is risky,' Gallant said, 'and too far back puts Melody's life in danger, then we do neither.'

'Doing neither is admitting defeat.'

'No. We ride the flanks. Out wide. That way, we're not following, we're abreast and keeping pace. . .

'Over tough going, rough ground. . .

'It was never going to be easy. But if they spot us – as they surely will – knowing there's a man riding on each flank will be as aggravatin' as ants in a bedroll. What do they do? Take time out to shake the bedding, rid themselves of the irritation? I think not. Judd will push on. His aim is to get rid of the little terrier that's itching to be up there in a Kansas City court of law, snapping at his brother's heels.'

'You realize we're discussing a crazy idea? Why follow at all, Gallant? So those two lead us to the cabin? No, we should take them now. Two of us, shock tactics. Come at them from the flanks – yes, that bit's good – hit them from the side, come in fast and hard out of the cold wet night—'

'We won't get the information we need from two dead men.'

'Then we make damn sure Judd's still breathing.'

McCrae whipped off his Stetson, slapped it against his thigh to get rid of the rainwater, planted it back on his head.

'I'll go left. You go right. I'll be riding a half circle, that gives me more ground to cover. You'll be in position first. When I'm level with 'em, I'll give the signal.'

'By whistling a few bars of *The Battle Cry of Freedom*?'

'Or maybe imitating an owl hoot.' McCrae tried a grin, but what emerged was forced, distracted. 'You know we're getting perilously close to riding that

101

kind of outlaw trail. . .

'. . . As we have in the past.' Gallant said.

'But this time it's for Melody, and by God I'd do it ten times over. . .

'Stick, shut up. You're stating the obvious, but as always, I don't know what I'd do without you. You've cleared my head, cut through the garbage. . .

But now he was talking to himself. McCrae had touched his horse with his spurs, lightly but with purpose, and was already riding hard down the wet, grassy slope.

'Remember, wait for the signal,' he called back over his shoulder, his words harsh even though muffled by the damp air. Then he was gone, the tails of his mackinaw flying, hitting the level ground close to the Judd gateposts and swinging right to follow the two men who had for some time been out of sight.

FOURTEEN

Gallant stayed on the high ground for the first hundred yards. At his flick of the reins the roan had set off at a grudging walk, quickly got used to the sheer pleasure of movement after hours spent dozing under the dripping trees, and eagerly picked up the pace to a fast trot. But the rain was a fine mist, not only soaking man and horse but making the grassy slopes treacherous in the darkness. As the ground fell away the grass lengthened, and now fronds with the toughness of fence-wire were threatening to snag forelegs and bring the big horse down. It snorted nervously, tossed it's head in protest as Gallant forced it onward with a touch of the spurs.

Still some way below them the packed earth of the trail, though slick with mud, would make for easier riding and give Judd and his strawboss an immediate advantage. Riding the flanks had been Gallant's idea. Tactically it made sense, but now he wondered if he should have heeded McCrae's warning of rough ground and rough riding forcing them to go slow. It was proving to be a massive handicap – and McCrae had further to travel and would be forced to ride recklessly.

So match him, Gallant thought savagely. Ride hard, trusting the roan to negotiate the ridges and the gullies and run straight and true on the slippery surface. It did its best, gallantly, and they made it without mishap to a point level with the trail but fifty yards or more away to the right. There the nature of the terrain changed, but not for the better: off the wet grass the roan was now picking a hazardous course through stands of trees, and open areas of rough scrub. In good light there would have been no difficulty, but the faint light enjoyed on the high ground had faded to nothing. The roan was pushing on semi-blind into the darkness. As for Gallant, he was forced to rely on his ears; listening hard for the beat of hoofs that would tell him when he had caught up with Judd and Kenny; listening, too, for McCrae's signal that would tell him it was time for action.

Whatever the hell that signal might be, Gallant thought, grinning savagely even as he listened, and waited.

Half a mile, maybe more. Then, out of the wet night, the signal that was impossible to be missed. It came as a harsh crack and a flash that in such darkness was like sheet lightning and told Gallant that McCrae was in no mood to waste time with subtlety. The brilliant muzzle flash, seen through the gossamer curtain of fine rain, was followed fractions of a second later by the brittle discharge of McCrae's six-gun. The shot was followed by a shrill, broken cry of anguish.

Before the flash had died, Gallant had his six-gun out. He spurred the roan out of the trees, pushed it at a dead run towards the unseen trail. Before he'd covered twenty yards there was a second flash, much brighter now because he was closing on the action. The crack of this shot had a different sound. Heavier. Judd or Kenny, returning fire – whichever man was left standing.

Gallant had thought himself down on a level with the trail. Not so. The ground suddenly fell away and the roan's dead run was slowed to a steep downhill scramble and slide, the horse sitting on its haunches and Gallant leaning back in the saddle. Two more shots. The detonations and flashes combined, coming to Gallant like forked lightning splitting age-old trees and revealing, a further twenty yards ahead, a water-filled ditch running parallel to the trail.

On the other flank, McCrae hadn't had it easy. In its meandering course from the Judd spread's gates the trail had gained height, forcing the journalist to finish his circuitous ride over rough ground with a push uphill. Somehow, in poor light and aiming upwards with a handgun inaccurate at any distance over twenty or so yards, he'd spotted the two men and managed to draw blood; he had winged one, then sensibly dropped back so that he and his horse were once again below the trail and out of sight.

Faced with that water-filled obstacle, Gallant leaned forward in the saddle, whispered soft words and took his roan in a raking leap over the deep ditch to land stiff-legged and sliding on the wet dirt of the trail. Out in the open, there was now enough eerie light to turn the scene before him into a flat and faded tintype; enough light to see that it was the strawboss, Dean Kenny, who had taken McCrae's bullet.

The lean man was painfully bowed in the saddle, both gloved hands fiercely gripping the horn. Mason Judd had moved his horse to the middle of the trail, shielding the helpless strawboss and positioning himself the better to watch for McCrae. The big rancher had been sitting in the saddle with pistol raised and cocked. The roan's explosive leap out of the darkness that brought Gallant into the fray changed the odds, but to little effect. Unperturbed, Judd merely glanced over his shoulder, shook his head, then used his knees to back his horse. This time he positioned himself so that neither McCrae nor Gallant could take him with a surprise attack.

'Enough,' Gallant said. 'It's over, Judd.'

'Call your friend in.'

'No need, he's not deaf.'

McCrae's horse brought the journalist up onto the trail in a mad scramble, stones and wet earth flying. It snorted, pawed the ground. Judd glared at McCrae with contempt, spat, turned to Gallant.

'We're going about our lawful business. You and McCrae—'

'McCrae?'

Judd sneered. 'Your names are known, rogues,

106

both of you, and here you attacked without warning and wounded a decent man.'

'Lawful business, you say? – after midnight, on a rain-swept night—'

'A man spending time in one of my cabins needs supplies.'

'That man is holding a young lawyer prisoner. She holds your brother's future in her hands.'

'The approaches from the north must be watched, I've lost valuable stock, there have been incursions by rustlers—'

'No. Your business tonight was to tell that feller the game's up, to kill the woman.'

'Maybe that was my business. Maybe yes, maybe no, and I say that because who of any importance is here to pass judgement? But that business itself is of no importance anyway, because now there's no need for it.'

Gallant, about to speak, frowned and shut his mouth. Judd was watching him. His florid face was wet with rain. In his eyes there was the glint of amusement; the gleam of supreme confidence. But as for his business, why no need for it? If there was no need, had another man been dispatched earlier? Had Judd been riding to check that the grisly task had been done? But, no, that could not be. There had been no other riders. They'd had Judd's property under constant watch from dusk to the moment Kenny and the rancher set out. Besides . . . the wording was wrong. Judd had said, 'But *now* there is no need for it.'

Why *now*?

Dean Kenny had sunk down in the saddle. There was no movement, no sign of life. The man was hanging on, slowly dying.

But what of Melody Lake?

'I think what our rich friend is telling us,' Stick McCrae said, 'is that the cabin is much closer than we suspected, and he'd put in place a contingency plan.'

'Halleluya, a newspaperman with brains,' Judd said – and he pouched his six-gun.

And in that instant Gallant understood, and felt failure as a tight band constricting his chest, clamping heart and lungs.

'The shots,' he said huskily.

'To be exact, McCrae's first shot,' Judd said.

'Damn you, are you saying McCrae's responsible?'

'He gave the signal.'

'Without knowing, he . . . Jesus Christ!'

Judd shrugged. 'His signal, my orders. Any shot, at any time of the day or night, raises the possibility of an attempt at rescue. That cannot happen, so Lake must die. You were right, Gallant, but for the wrong reason. For you and McCrae, it really is all over.'

FIFTEEN

For Gallant and McCrae, those final words spoken by Judd cleared the air.

They pushed on for the cabin with their minds washed clean of all argument, all speculation. They rode at a fast canter, judging that pace to be a good balance between recklessness and caution. The rain had ceased. A freshening breeze was blowing in from the north, whipping away the white breath of the straining horses. Thick clouds had rolled away, and pale moonlight glinted on dripping branches and the slick mud of the trail that wound ahead through timber and scrub to . . . to what?

Dean Kenny had toppled from his horse, dead from shock and the loss of blood, which soaked into the wet earth. They'd left Judd struggling to drape his strawboss belly down over the man's chestnut mare, the rancher spitting curses as he used a rawhide thong to lash Kenny's wrists to ankles under the horse's belly. The last they'd seen of them in the wet gloom, Judd had been riding back to his spread leading the mare with its gruesome burden.

All right, Gallant thought. Half-a-dozen terse words had cleared the air. *It's over. You're finished.* Or words to that effect. And their effect was that he and McCrae were no longer thinking in circles looking for the solution to a problem that had always been unclear, because according to Judd that problem had been taken out of their hands. But why should they believe him? Was it over – or had it just begun? The answer lay a mile or so ahead up the trail, but any thoughts on what that might be – the life or death of a young woman – Gallant was forced to leave until later.

Out of the dark night, he had fresh problems to occupy his mind.

'You hear what I hear, Gallant?' McCrae called.

Gallant laughed grimly, slowed to let McCrae alongside, the narrow trail forcing the lean journalist to ride close enough to brush thighs, clash stirrups.

'If the man guarding Melody heard your shots,' Gallant said, 'so did the men in the bunkhouse. That contingency plan was double ended. Distant gunfire would have the fatal pull of a trigger at one end, men piling out at the other, spoiling for a fight. My guess is they met Judd on the trail.'

'So he would have sent one of them back with his dead foreman,' McCrae panted, 'and what we're hearing is a wild bunch of men hot on our trail.'

'Except we're not Judd's concern unless we get in his way. He's riding to make sure the crucial part of his contingency plan went without a hitch.'

'And we're heading in the same direction in the faint hope his man couldn't bring himself to kill a young woman in cold blood. Look, those men aren't going to catch us. When we get to the cabin there's ways we can muddy the waters, spoil Judd's party.'

'An interesting thought. Got any ideas?'

'If she's dead. . .' McCrae broke off, the hand holding the reins clamped on the horn as he flapped with the other to swipe splashes of mud from his face, his mouth. He looked across at Gallant with narrowed, angry eyes. 'If he *has* killed her, this Judd man, if Melody *is* dead – then what we do is send him merrily on his way to join her, then drag both bodies into the woods and sit back and watch the fun.'

'You should be writing fiction, I hear there's money to be made in dime novels.'

'Judd needs a story for his brother, Gallant. We give him an empty cabin, he's left with nothing to tell.'

For several minutes they rode on without speaking. Their horses were high-stepping, kicking up mud. The hard north wind was in their faces, causing eyes to water and wet clothing to cling to already chilled skin. They knew the cabin was close – close being open to different interpretations, and in the weak light there was no guarantee they wouldn't ride straight on by – but McCrae's words had set Gallant thinking. It had seemed that with Melody lost forever there was nothing left for them, but if she was beyond help there was still a corrupt politician who should be stopped in his tracks.

And then there was Frank Lake.

'Melody has a grandfather,' he said, raising his voice to be heard. 'For his sake we need to get her back to Kansas City.'

'Talk sense, Gallant. That's a three-, four-day ride. Alive, OK, but if we've lost her all we can do is bury her here and mark the grave.'

'With her work unfinished, a corrupt Kansas City politician will be home and dry. For Melody, and all she stood for, that cannot be allowed.'

'*Stood* for? You writing her off so soon?'

'A slip of the tongue, don't you know?' Gallant said, flashing a mirthless grin.

Using the end of his reins as a quirt, he pushed his roan from fast canter to gallop and pulled away from McCrae. He was blinking hard, the wind stinging his face. His flat-brimmed hat was hanging on his shoulders, his wet hair flying like a pale battle pennant. He grinned at the thought, turned his head to the side, whipped his collar up to shield his ear from the icy blast, somehow kept his eyes skinned for a run-down line cabin. On the edge of the Flint Hills, he had always reckoned it would be bounded on three sides by thick forest. But if he wasn't to miss it, he thought ruefully, everything depended on which way the open side faced.

A few hundred yards of fast riding with the woods thickening on either side, and then the trail split. At that Y fork Gallant slowed the roan, cursing softly. He squinted ahead, then to the left. The pale moonlight was slanting through the trees. The left branch of the

112

trail appeared to have been little used, the grass long and thick. So what was it for, where did it go?'

'Try it,' McCrae called, catching up and dragging his horse to a fierce halt alongside Gallant's roan. He hooked a thumb over his shoulder. 'They're closing on us, Gallant. We're running out of time.'

The left fork took a sharp bend fifty yards further on. Pushing through the long grass, they rode into a clearing. Gallant saw at once that he had been wrong. The line cabin was backed up against the woods, but clear on three sides. Warped split logs, a rusted tin roof, one door, one window. No light. No sign of life. No horse at the sagging hitch rail.

'If he's killed her,' Gallant said quietly, drawing rein and sliding from the saddle, 'he'd be heading for home. He didn't pass us, so if there's no other way back to the spread. . .'

'He must be lying on the floor, at the very least as sick as a dog,' Melody Lake said. She'd come riding out of the woods on a ragged bay gelding, dark hair blowing in the wind, her eyes flashing fire. 'I've been cooped up in this cabin for half my adult life, Gallant, what the hell took you so long?'

SIXTEEN

'I heard the shots, knew my life was hanging by a slender thread. The unshaven lout came at me grinning and drawing his six-gun, so I kicked him where it hurts the most, then snatched his rifle from the table. He was down on his knees, groaning. I gripped the rifle by the barrel, in two hands, used it like an axe, a cleaver. There was a lot of blood. By the sound of bone cracking I think I broke his neck.'

She'd told that part of her story in haste, showing them the rifle – a Henry repeater, bloodstained but undamaged – with which she'd tried to remove the guard's head. Then, fearful of being caught cold by the pursuing riders, they'd circled the cabin and ridden into the woods, in line abreast but spaced so they could work their way through the trees. The noise of the horses crashing through the undergrowth and snorting with effort drowned all other sounds, but Gallant knew that Judd and his men would have reached the cabin, would have kicked open the door and be inside looking down at another dead man.

They rode for ten minutes, sprayed by rainwater from disturbed branches that snapped back like whips. Darkness became wan light in an instant as they rode out of the woods into a glade, a grassy hollow encircled by trees and with a central, murky pool with crusted surface algae glowing green in the moonlight.

They drew to a breathless halt; to the creak of leather, the clink of bridle metal as Melody Lake dismounted and stretched luxuriously.

'I've been locked up for too long. Pacing a wooden cell with men who've not heard of soap and water. Freedom, fresh air, the land washed clean by rain – this is bliss.'

'Half your life, I believe that's what you said.'

'I might have exaggerated, but that wasn't one of your English mansions, Gallant. You should try it for size some time.'

'Damned if I will.' He grinned. 'But, given that dismal accommodation, you've managed to keep your attire in good shape. Dark skirt just a bit stained, tastefully patterned neckerchief over a crisp white shirt. . .'

'It was once.'

'Shiny boots —'

'Now badly scuffed.'

'But showing class, nevertheless. From what I heard you were dressed in your best for some routine appointment as a legal eagle, never made it because our friend Chet Eagan snatched you off a city street.'

115

'With help. Without warning. If I'd been given just half a chance, they'd never have made it.'

'And if we don't get out of here now,' Stick McCrae said, 'we won't live to see another dawn. When Judd finds that man with his neck broken he won't waste time, he'll come after us. . .'

'I beg to differ.'

'Though it pains me to say so after his poor showing, I do agree with Gallant,' Melody said. 'Judd knows exactly where we're going. The ride to Kansas City will take us two, three days. Why try to hunt us down through dark, wet woodland, with the added risk of ambush? He and his men can get a good night's sleep back at the spread, then take their time riding us down on the open plains in bright daylight.'

'We'll have to discuss that cruel accusation of a poor showing at a later date, don't you know,' Gallant said, 'because if Judd is going to spend several hours snoring, we've got the opportunity to gallop a few miles, open up some space. Judd won't take part in the chase, but at daylight we'll be in a desperate race to stay ahead of Chet and Gord Eagan, and the man I humbled at a moonlit creek: a fellow called Largo, who will bear a definite grudge. The more miles we can put between us. . .'

'My turn to say no.' Melody was shaking her head. 'You two are wearing coats sodden by hours of rain, all I've got, as you pointed out, is a thin white shirt. If Judd can get his head down, so can we – for an hour or two. And I happen to know that in that cabin there are good thick coats, several of them, put there for the use of ranch hands on line duty.'

'You know,' Gallant said, 'these outpourings of pure common sense make me wish I'd had you riding alongside me from the start. Of course, as it's you I was looking for, and nobody can be in two places at the same time, especially someone being held prisoner, incarcerated in damnable. . .'

'Shut up, Gallant,' Melody Lake said, but as she swung back into the saddle it was obvious from the way she turned her head away that she was smothering a grin.

They were mounted and ready to go, but in too much of a rush. Gallant exercised caution. He stopped them with a raised hand as they rode up the slope out of the hollow, held them on the edge of the woods in moon-cast shadows. In the silence they could hear the steady drip of rainwater, the clatter of branches and fiercer showers as the wind swept across the treetops. Of wildlife, of birds, there was no sight or sound. They had more sense than men, Gallant reckoned. Curled up in nests and lairs, snoozing the night away.

The thought of such comfort reminded him of Melody's thin white shirt. He offered her his sodden coat. She refused tactfully, pointing out that it was better to be dry and cold than wet and cold.

And Gallant's caution was justified. There was a muffled shout from the direction of the cabin. Words indistinguishable, but more calls were followed by a

117

short bark of laughter and then the rumble of hoof-beats, swiftly fading.

Give it five more minutes, Gallant told them.

'Even then,' McCrae said, 'there's the risk that he's left a man in the cabin.'

'Everything from now on is a risk,' Gallant said, 'but I don't see danger here. We heard them ride away. Judd will do exactly as Melody said, he and his men will get some rest, then hunt us down in daylight.'

Once through the woods, Gallant took it upon himself to dismount and approach the cabin. McCrae and Lake split up, taking their horses to either end of the hitch rail, McCrae with his six-gun drawn, Lake holding the dead guard's rifle.

The door opened to Gallant's kick. He stepped swiftly to one side, turned and flattened himself against the wall.

'Clear,' McCrae called.

The cabin was empty.

Inside, Melody Lake took over. Hell, Gallant thought, this has been her home for days on end, and he watched as she located matches, struck one and applied the flame to a lamp's wick. She lowered the glass, light flared, provided a circle of illumination. Gallant saw bunk beds with tossed blankets against the back wall, several short, thick mackinaws on wooden hooks, a table with cups, plates, open food tins with jagged tops, several rickety straight-backed chairs, and on the dirt floor a dark stain, the drag marks made by a dead man's heels.

There was a black, pot-bellied iron stove. It was warm to Gallant's touch.

'You two take the bunks,' he said, moving to shut the door. 'For a bed, I'll pile some of those coats on the floor by the stove. I don't know the time now, it's after midnight but—' McCrae tugged on a chain leading to his pocket, brandished a battered turnip watch. Flipped it open.

'Two hours from now will take us to an hour before dawn,' he said.

Gallant nodded. 'Ideal. They won't move that early. I'll make sure you two are awake.'

Melody Lake was already moving. The dead guard's rifle clattered on to the table, back from where it had been snatched. She scooped mackinaws from the hooks, tossed several at Gallant's feet, shrugged into the cleanest she could find and climbed agilely on to the top bunk.

Gallant looked at McCrae, rolled his eyes.

'Did you have a choice?'

'It's hers, and welcome to it,' McCrae said, 'but I do have a word of warning. Gord Eagan was a wartime sniper. He's an expert with the .451 Whitworth rifle, I hear he regularly hit targets at close to 2,000 yards. They'll come after us, we know that, and we're prepared to run for our lives. Our big problem is, this is Kansas, a land of flat prairies, which means we can run but we can't easily hide. They get within a mile of us, Gord Eagan and his Whitworth muzzleloader will pick us off like sitting ducks.'

119

PART THREE

SEVENTEEN

When dawn broke they were ten miles north of the cabin and riding spread out on a wide trail beaten into the earth by the herds of cattle being driven from Texas to the Kansas railheads. They'd breakfasted on jerky and sourdough bread washed down with water Melody drew from a wooden butt at the side of the cabin. That same butt had filled their water canteens. Now, low in the eastern sky, the sun was a blinding light bringing with it, even that early, a welcome spreading warmth. Another mile and Melody Lake had discarded the mackinaw she'd worn to keep warm while she slept, tying it behind her saddle. There was no wind, other than that they themselves created as they pushed north.

Good light and no wind, Gallant mused, with misgivings. If he had a man acting as spotter they were ideal conditions for snipers, in any war you'd care to name. Given a clear target. . .

He looked across, at her white shirt, called to Melody Lake.

'Taking that jacket off was a bad idea.'

'It stank, Gallant.'

'I take that to mean the jacket. But if you'd put up with the smell you'd look like me and McCrae. That would give you a one in three chance of staying alive when the shooting starts.'

'OK, the white shirt marks me out, identifies me,' she agreed, at once understanding, 'but a rifleman capable of hitting a target at 2,000 yards is at his limit. I've been keeping an eye out. There's no sign of pursuit. If they're even five miles back and we're keeping up a steady ten, twelve miles an hour – which we are – closing that gap will be difficult.'

'Spoken like a lawyer. A reasoned argument, but in a courtroom there'd be an opposing viewpoint. What d'you think, Stick?'

McCrae was riding out to the left. He said, 'We can't argue with facts.'

'Ah, but lawyers do just that.'

'Maybe so, but I've also been keeping a watch. You know what the land is like. Flat as a frying pan this side of the Flint Hills. Anything moves, jack rabbit, coyote, men on horseback, we'd see them. But there's nothing.'

'Maybe they slept too well,' Gallant said. 'But Melody pointed out yesterday that they have no need to rush. Night falls, we'll be forced to stop, rest. . .'

'Maybe we should stop in the daytime.' McCrae

said, 'and do the riding at night. Even the best of snipers couldn't hit a barn door in the dark.'

They pushed on, keeping the horses to the same mile-eating canter, with it the comforting knowledge that pursuers would struggle to catch up. The endless, flat landscape made it easy to maintain that pace. Like a frying pan was right, Gallant thought, though a griddle was a better analogy. But if so, it was a griddle with imperfections, for here and there on that monotonous Kansas landscape there were stands of trees looking forlorn, or a rise that managed to reach the giddy height of a hundred feet.

He'd mentioned stopping at night, but Gallant was well aware that if they were to be pushed hard then horses need regular rest periods. So far there had been none, and they'd now covered a good twelve miles. McCrae's idea of resting during the day, riding during the hours of darkness, had some merit, but it would need to be discussed. So, rest the horses as soon as possible, toss that idea around. . .

A mile ahead of them and a little to the west of the broad trail the land rose to a hillock topped with boulders, some sparse scrub. Maybe the start of the foothills leading to the Flints. Much closer, but on the eastern side, there was a dense stand of tall aspen. The trees would provide shade, and cover, but to Gallant they bore another advantage. Viewed from the trail they were directly in line with the dazzling light of the rising sun. Lake and McCrae had seen nothing moving behind them, but with the

Whitworth rifle Gord Eagan didn't need to be close, or exposed. Behind rocks, rifle resting on the natural support, he could take a bead from 1,000 yards, pull the trigger – job done. But he could never pull off that shot if he was looking through the leaf sight, or whatever the hell kind he was using, directly into the sun's brilliant orb.

'Over there,' Gallant shouted to his two outriders. 'We'll take a break in those trees, rest the horses, discuss Stick's idea.'

Melody was the first to move. Young and feisty, Gallant thought, grinning as he watched. She put spurs to the dead man's ragged gelding, cut across the trail in front of Gallant and McCrae. Her shirt blindingly white in the sunlight, she threw them a cheery wave and headed for the trees at full gallop.

Pure luck, Gallant thought later. If she hadn't moved fast, the thin, hexagonal bullet from the Whitworth would have ended her life. There was no sound, the distance was too great, but the location of the rifleman was marked by a faint puff of gunsmoke. Gord Eagan wasn't firing into the sun. He was firing south from the rocky rise a mile ahead of the trio. Judd's men hadn't overslept, they'd risen early. When Gallant, McCrae and Melody Lake left the cabin, their pursuers were already miles ahead of them, and heading north to set up a simple, planned ambush.

EIGHTEEN

'Impasse,' Gallant said. 'What you Americans call a Mexican stand-off.'

They were in the woods, down off their mounts. The sunlight was slanting through the trees, hitting all three of them with brilliant shafts of warm light in which insects danced. Melody was sitting cross-legged on parched grass, dead leaves, her back against a smooth trunk. Stick McCrae had walked to the northern edge of the trees and was gazing towards the distant rising ground, the rocks from behind which the gunman had fired that single shot.

'Stick can look, but he won't see anything,' Gallant said, nodding towards McCrae. 'We're pinned down, so why should they make a move? All they need do is sit back. The longer they keep you here, a prisoner without the need of a cabin's walls, the closer Emerson Judd gets to his office in Washington.'

'I don't understand you. You're the eternal optimist, now acting pessimistic, when actually it's not all bleak,' Melody said. 'That Whitworth's a muzzle-loader. I can make a run for it, go out fast from the eastern side of these trees instead of back on to the trail – sometime soon we've got to turn to the north-east anyway. He'll have reloaded by now, and be ready, but if he misses with the first shot I'll stand a good chance of getting clear.'

Gallant pushed his hat on to his back, ran fingers through his hair.

'No, that's not the answer.'

Walking back in, McCrae said, 'I think he would miss, and that's if he manages to get a shot off. A sniper's rifle needs firm support – a bipod, or convenient rocks with a folded bandanna for a pad. If he's settled, lined up in one direction, then has to change position and take fresh aim on a fast-moving target. . .' He visualized it, shook his head. 'No, not possible.'

'And not the answer,' Gallant insisted. 'Melody goes out that side and runs for it, there'll be no missed shots. No need for 'em. They'll come racing down off that high ground and cut her off.'

Melody nodded. 'Yes, you're right, of course. And them already being ahead of us, not behind as we thought, has changed everything.'

'Judd used his brains, came up with the answer and put his men in an unassailable position,' McCrae said. 'They can sit tight, do nothing. The way north is effectively blocked.'

'It is, yes, but I won't accept defeat,' Melody said. She rose to her feet, stood with arms folded, visibly disturbed. 'Gallant? Come on, man, there must be some way out of this fix.'

He'd wandered over to his roan and was taking his water canteen from the saddle-bag. Also taking his time, and looking out of the trees, back the way they had come. When he turned to face them the shafts of sunlight slanting in behind him turned his blond hair into a golden crown.

'But you should accept it,' he said. Deep in thought, he was picking his words with care. 'Accept it, make a point of showing them that you've given up, the game is theirs.'

'Well I'll be damned,' Melody said, glaring. 'Is that the Born Gallant who I helped ride away from Salvation Creek, the man who. . .'

'Give McCrae your shirt.'

'What?'

'We'll turn away, close our eyes. Give him your hat, and that bright neckerchief that'll look glorious in the bright morning sun. Give him that unkempt gelding you stole. . .'

'Oh, it's stole now, is it?'

'Well, yes, you're a horse thief and a killer,' Gallant said, using the palm of his hand to dash water from his chin, watching her with laughing blue eyes as he stowed the canteen. 'The game's up, you've accepted it, and you're returning to Eldorado with your tail between your legs.'

For a long, tense minute there was silence. Then McCrae nodded slowly. Melody was looking intently at Gallant, at first with her head cocked on one side, then with a slow smile she unfolded her arms, stood straight, fluffed her dark hair.

'So when McCrae's heading back to El Dorado wearing a woman's shirt,' she said softly, 'what will we be doing?'

'Dealing with the opposition. Boot on the other foot. To go after you – or even to return like whipped curs to the Judd mansion – they'll have to come this way. We'll be ready in deep cover, and them out in the open? Hell, they won't stand a chance.'

NINETEEN

'If they're up there using field glasses,' Melody said, 'they'll tumble to the ruse in an instant.'

Gallant was watching McCrae. Already a couple of hundred yards away, he was riding down the trail towards El Dorado in a manner that would scream of defeat. He was keeping the gelding to a slow trot, and cutting a disconsolate figure in the saddle. This was a woman, he was implying, who had discarded one failed plan aimed at getting her back to Kansas City, and had yet to come up with a better one. And by keeping the gelding to little more than walking pace McCrae was making it obvious to the watchers on the high ground that if they moved fast they could very quickly get rid of the one obstacle standing between Emerson Judd and his dreams of power.

That Gord Eagan would simply shoot the man impersonating Melody Lake out of the saddle was a risk they'd had to take. Their justification had been that by making it appear that Melody was heading back to El Dorado, they had defused the situation, taken away most of the urgency.

'They're sure to be using field-glasses, because Eagan would need a spotter,' Gallant said. 'But McCrae's not built like a bruiser. I've got clothes hangers wider than his shoulders. . .'

'That's cruel.'

'And not strictly true, but you know what I mean: he's of slim build, and he's doing all he can to look even smaller. Your shirt, your hat, that neckerchief a splash of many bright colours in the sunlight. No, even with strong glasses they'll take a quick look, see what we want 'em to see, and come running.'

'Not kill him with a single shot?'

'We've discussed that, taken the gamble.'

'Stick McCrae certainly has. OK, but even if we've got them fooled, why would they be in a hurry to follow me? Time's running out. By going back to El Dorado I'm wasting more, and that's playing into their hands.'

'It looks that way, yes, but they cannot let you out of their sight. This could be some kind of double bluff. Also, from El Dorado there's the railroad to Florence – though I haven't a clue if the line continues north towards Kansas City. If it doesn't, there's always the stage, either from El Dorado or Florence. They can't risk losing you.'

'There's something else they can't do.'

'Go on.'

'They can't go after the rider they think is me without dealing with the two in the woods – the two they believe to be you and McCrae. If they did, they'd have armed opponents ahead and behind.'

'True, and nobody wants to be the dead meat in a six-gun sandwich.'

They were talking, and watching. As soon as McCrae had climbed aboard the ragged gelding and set off for El Dorado they'd moved to the extreme western fringe of the woods. From there they had a clear view of the rising ground surmounted by the rocks used by Gord Eagan, for cover, and support for his Whitworth rifle.

It had occurred to Gallant – and he had pointed this out with some amusement to Melody Lake – that they really had no idea how many men had set out early from the Judd spread, how many were up there concealed by the rocks. What if, he'd said, there's just Eagan and his big gun?

Unlikely, Lake had said. And Gallant had agreed that her guess that at the most two or three of Judd's men would be with Eagan was probably right. But Judd had been banking on Eagan picking Melody Lake off from a distance. That objective had failed.

Gallant had his Winchester. Before McCrae rode out, Lake had plucked the Henry repeater from the gelding's saddle boot, inspected it closely to see if the violent impact with her guard's neck had damaged it and announced it serviceable. It had a full magazine; Gallant had a full magazine and spare shells in his pockets. They had picked their positions with care. They would fire kneeling, left shoulder against a tree trunk, and elbows and knees providing firm natural support.

130

'Movement,' Gallant warned.

'Seen it. There's just two of them. You should feel insulted. Judd can't rate you and McCrae very highly.'

'Why d'you think I play the silly ass? Underestimating the capabilities of the opposition has led to the downfall of armies.'

'You sound like a pompous general with a silly moustache and a puffed-out chest. May I point out that Eagan and his pal are moving fast. What are we targeting, horses or men?'

'Neither, just yet. I'm not saying wait till you see the whites of their eyes, but we'll let 'em get closer. They know we're in here and, as you pointed out, they think it's me and McCrae. Just about now, in my past life as a soldier, a military commander would be calling out, "Steady, men, hold fast!".'

'Hmm,' Melody said, 'and wasn't it a wounded Lieutenant-Colonel Inglis who cried out in a famous Peninsular War battle, "Die hard, 57th, die hard!" '

'Bless my soul,' Gallant said, 'she's not just a lawyer.' Then he grinned. 'He did indeed, a fine chap, but our aim, young lady, is to come out of this alive and kicking.'

The two men they were discussing were already down from the high ground. The once-white Stetson Gallant had seen in Salvation Creek marked out Eagan. They'd emerged from the cover of the rocks, brought their horses down the slope at a breakneck gallop, then turned south. They were eating away the distance between the high ground and the aspen grove, the pounding hoofs leaving behind a plume of dust that hung in the still air. Then, without slowing the pace, they split up and swung off the trail. The gap between them widening rapidly, they headed straight for the trees. They were riding flattened along their mount's outstretched necks. Both horses had long, flaring manes. All Gallant could see of the riders was their knees and elbows out to the sides, and the crowns of their Stetsons.

'They've done this before,' he said. 'They're makin' themselves impossible targets. Can't believe it's an English aristocrat saying this but, sadly, it has to be the horses. I'll take the one on the left.' And, elbow resting on his knee, the rifle's stock cuddled against his cheek, he fired the first shot.

Even then, he was too slow. His finger was beginning to squeeze the trigger when both Eagan and his companion kicked their feet from the stirrups and tumbled sideways from the saddle. They hit the ground rolling. The horses at once veered sharply and cantered towards the trail, empty stirrups flapping, heads high and turned to keep trailing reins to the side.

Gallant's shot, unable to be stopped, went winging towards the Flint Hills.

Melody Lake had held her fire, possibly because she hadn't the stomach for killing horses in cold blood. She was more exposed than Gallant. Banking on the men never getting close, she had chosen an opening in the trees that would give her an unrestricted view. But she was wearing Stick McCrae's mackinaw, and her long dark hair was tucked up under his hat. A man rushing the trees, snatching swift glances in the heat of battle, would see not Melody Lake, but Stick McCrae – and McCrae was the man who had fired the shot that killed Judd's strawboss, Dean Kenny.

Gord Eagan would want to avenge that killing. He would also recall the way his brother, Chet, had been damn near scalped by Born Gallant on the gallery of Guthrie Flint's house. And even as they tumbled from their saddles, Gallant recognized the second man as Largo, the swarthy, unshaven outlaw he had humbled at that cold, moonlit creek.

Two men, under orders from Judd, but also bearing grudges.

Almost as soon as they hit the ground Eagan and Largo were up on their feet, charging towards the trees in fast, swerving, jinking runs. Out wide when they abandoned their mounts, they were now narrowing the angle, bearing down on the position where Gallant and Lake lay in wait. Running fast, swerving, impossible targets for those armed with rifles, as they came on they fired a volley of snap shots from their six-guns. Wild, but effective. The bullets kicked up dust and leaves, chipped white splinters from tree trunks. Gallant and Lake were driven back into deeper cover – and Gallant was forced to the galling admission that he'd ignored his own warning: handling a rifle in thick timber is like playing baseball underwater.

Their attackers had almost reached the trees.

'Back, move back,' Gallant yelled. He waited a precious second, two seconds, saw Melody spring to her feet and run. Then, before obeying his own order, he stood and threw his rifle overhand at Largo in a deadly vertical spin. The outlaw was just entering the woods. The hand holding his six-gun was extended, the other arm raised to sweep aside saplings, thin branches. The butt of Gallant's rifle hit him on the right temple. He stumbled backwards, slammed into a tree, began to go down. Even then, dazed, eyes glazed, he managed to fire a single wild shot.

But Gallant was already away and clear, crashing through the trees

Ahead of him Melody, fleet of foot, was threading her way nimbly through the aspen trees and ground-level scrub they had hoped to use for life-saving cover. Gallant, cursing his stupidity in stopping to deal with Largo, saw that she was in danger of being caught by Gord Eagan. Once close enough, that man would stop, steady himself, and shoot her in the back.

'Gord Eagan, over here!' Gallant yelled.

He drew his six-gun, slowed his pace.

Eagan's curses turned the Kansas air blue. He flung an arm around a tree trunk and used it to spin towards Gallant. The gaunt face with the fierce dragoon moustache was contorted with fury. Melody Lake, finding herself now behind Eagan, also turned quickly. Her rifle was cocked, held down at waist level, her eyes darting from Eagan to Gallant.

'Hate to say it, Eagan,' Gallant called, 'but as of

134

now you need eyes in the back of your head.'

The answer was a well-aimed shot that sent bark chippings into Gallant's face. He swore, staggered back, eyes stinging. Another shot rang out. Through misted vision he saw Lake duck for cover, Eagan seize his chance and make a run for it through the trees.

But he won't go far, Gallant thought grimly. Their ruse had run its course. Eagan now knew that the lawyer he had orders to kill was not on her way back to El Dorado, but here in these woods.

Then two shots rang out behind Gallant. A mighty blow struck his boot. Pain knifed through his leg all the way to his hip. He went down, teeth clenched, rolled in the crisp dead leaves, heard Melody Lake yell, 'Gallant, stay down, stay still.'

Dropping like a stone had put Gallant out of Largo's line of sight. Melody was thinking on her feet, leaving Eagan to run and moving in fast on Gallant. She could see that his rifle had dealt the outlaw a crippling blow. Largo was back on his feet, advancing, but clinging to trees for support. He was shaking his head like a terrier with a rat. It was a vain attempt to clear blurred vision.

Again Largo fired. But his six-gun was quivering like a water diviner's hazel stick. The shot kicked up dirt yards wide. Melody Lake was now almost up with Gallant, maybe thirty yards from the outlaw. Clearly, she felt that was close enough. Still holding the rifle at waist level, she gave Largo the briefest of glances and fired a single shot.

'That's a circus trick, if ever I saw one,' Gallant

said. He had his head down, and was clutching his ankle.

'So maybe I chose the wrong career.'

'D'you get him?'

'He's down. He's not moving.'

'So now there's just Eagan.'

'Forget Eagan. If you'd been listening instead of feeling sorry for yourself you'd have heard McCrae coming back up the trail at speed. Pony Express has got nothing on Stick. I'll look at your wound, leave the intrepid journalist to keep the enemy at bay.'

'You love this, don't you?'

'As long as it's you getting shot, not me.'

She knelt down, wrenched off his boot.

'You're a big softy, Gallant. It's not even bleeding. The bullet glanced off, you'll have a purple bruise on your ankle bone, might need a walking stick when you're an old man.'

She was still on her knees when a rattle of gunfire jerked her head up.

'Different sound, different direction.' Gallant said, easing his bruised foot back into his boot.

'Yes. That's Stick, from the open ground. I don't hear a return of fire.'

'Dead men find that difficult to do.'

'But we want Eagan alive.'

'Do we?'

'There are two of them, Gallant. We need to know his brother's whereabouts.'

He nodded, grabbed her outstretched hand and climbed to his feet.

'Yes, we do,' he said. 'Forewarned is forearmed. Because if Chet Eagan's where I think he is, we're in for a torrid time in Kansas City.'

TWENTY

Three days later. Evening, the sinking sun a sliver of cold light stretching above the western hills, dusk bringing with it a knee-high white mist over the prairie, through which their mounts plodded listlessly. Bone weary, coated in trail dust and with the buildings of Kansas City a line of misshapen blocks on a hazy skyline, Gallant suggested to Stick McCrae that he should ride into town on his own.

'You're the only one of us likely to make it into town in one piece,' he said, moistening dry lips. 'Journalist, always sniffing for a scoop, people expect you to pop up out of nowhere and make a nuisance of yourself. That includes Judd. He'll have someone keeping a wary eye on you, but you'll come to no harm. It's people like you who keep his name up there in bold headlines. As for me, despite all my efforts to look like a footloose drifter, I still stand out like a red-nosed clown at a funeral.'

'We'll get there in the end,' Melody Lake told

McCrae, 'but using two words as our guide: circum-spect, and circuitous.'

'Yeah, and crafty's another,' McCrae said. 'Admit it, you've got me as the terrified deer tied in the moonlit clearing while you two get a clear run in from another direction.'

'And no need to tell you which route we're taking,' Melody said, grinning. 'I tell you, this English clown just can't stay away from the place.'

With Stick McCrae a lone, silhouetted rider heading for the city, Gallant and Melody Lake pointed their horses' noses to the north-east. An hour's steady riding saw them cutting on to a trail Gallant recog-nized, despite night drawing in: it was the one he had taken on his ride south to El Dorado. Another couple of miles and the remaining light showed him the long grassy slope of the hillside down which Karl Danson had ridden to where Gallant had waited impatiently in the trees.

Then, quite soon afterwards, it was Salvation Creek. Ahead of them as they drew their horses to a halt the lights of the Last Chance saloon, spilling out past the half-drawn hanging blanket serving as a door. The pool of yellow light barely reached across the trail, didn't touch the foot of the road that wound up through the shabby houses. There, in the darkness of the night, it was replaced by the glimmer from oil lamps seen dimly through filthy glass windows. Deathly stillness hung like a cloud. A whisper of sound from the saloon. The cry of a night bird.

'It being late,' Gallant said into the silence, 'I think we should put up at the nearest hotel. Proprietor Karl Danson. Deceased.' He lifted a hand, pointed at the barn where he had kept his roan stabled alongside Danson's. 'I call that place my bedroom. Stayed there one night. I'm drawn to it, but the present company means something more than a bed of straw is required. We'll put the horses there, in the barn, but as for us. . .'

Again the wave of the hand.

'There?' A crooked grin of disbelief from Melody. 'That's not a . . . well, I didn't expect a hotel in Salvation Creek, of all places, but that's not even a rooming-house.'

'But it is . . . was . . .Danson's house.'

'And you've got the key?'

'I've got a foot, a boot, and the lock is flimsy.'

It was the door jamb, not the lock, that splintered suddenly to Gallant's weighted kick. His bullet-bruised ankle gave way, almost putting him down. He half limped, half fell into the room. Recovering, he looked at the oil lamp on the table, fumbled in his pocket for matches. The lamp's dry wick sputtered to the match's flame, caught, flared as he replaced the sooted glass chimney. Shadows slunk away. The room was as he'd left it; as Danson had left it, tidy, and walked out, never to return.

'Those bunks will do us for a night,' Gallant said gruffly as Melody followed him into the circle of light. 'I'll see to the horses. Somewhere you'll find grub. We can eat it cold, save lighting that monstrosity of a stove.'

'And while that's going on,' she said, moving to the table by the window, 'you can tell me all about the man called Danson and where he fits in. . .'

She got no further.

The still open door slammed back at yet another kick. Melody spun, eyes wide. Gallant dropped into a crouch, slapped a hand to his six-gun – then straightened with a disgusted grunt. The newcomer was unarmed, carried with him the foetid stink of stale alcohol.

'Jake Arkle, bartender,' he said, for Melody's benefit. Then, to Arkle. 'Like to listen in to private conversations, don't you? Send men to their deaths. Quint and Largo. You know they're both dead?'

'Death's why I'm here,' Arkle said.

He closed the door with a casual backheel. Lamplight shone on his greasy scalp. His black beard straggled on to his grubby undershirt, the same red suspenders held up the same black trousers which now bore more stains accumulated from unmentionable sources. Hands thrust deep into pockets, he leaned back against the door, turned his attention to Melody.

'Your grandpa,' he said. 'Seems he came to a violent end. Outside his front door, shotgun fired by person or persons unknown.' He grinned. 'That last's a bit of lawyer speak, so a clever young woman gets the message. Means the killer vamoosed, got clean away.'

141

Her eyes had narrowed as the news hit home. She pursed her lips, seemed to draw a shaky breath, then she shook her head. Her sudden smile was pleasant, her words scathing.

'That doesn't explain how you know my name, you greasy little man. Nor why you're here. Were you paid well to come here spreading sadness?'

'I told you. Death's here, by special delivery.'

His hands were still in his pants' pockets. Suddenly the light in his eyes darkened, the eyelids flickered. His right hand came out fast, a lightning draw made easy because the gun had always been in his hand. It was a Remington Elliot .22 pocket pistol, walnut butt, ring for a trigger.

For me, Gallant thought in a flash. He'll see her as a frail young woman, dismiss her, see me as the danger. As the pistol came up Gallant took a fast sideways step, again going for his Peacemaker. Once again he was let down by his weakened ankle – but this time the injury saved his life. The first of the derringer's five shots sounded like an old man weakly spitting into a tin cuspidor, but a bullet from a short-barrelled pocket pistol can end a man's life. This one simply raked Gallant's shoulder as his ankle twisted. He toppled, reached desperately for the stove. The bullet ricocheted from iron with a clang and a whine, thudded into a wall. He saw the tiny pistol's muzzle swing towards him, the stained-tooth grin on Jake Arkle's bearded face.

'Arkle!'

His name, shouted loud and clear by Melody Lake,

distracted the bartender. His finger was stayed in the ring trigger. His eyes flicked away from Gallant towards the young woman. As they did so, Melody said, 'Catch this, little man,' and with a wide swing of her left arm she swept the lighted oil lamp off the table and flung it at his face.

It hit the centre of Jake Arkle's forehead. The glass chimney shattered, the oil reservoir split. Flame caught the spilled oil, flickered, flared.

Arkle howled. The Remington pistol flew into the air as both his hands slapped at his face. But the pain there was from the lamp's impact. Future agony would come from the burning oil spilling on to his shoulders and chest, as for an instant it seemed as if he must go up in flames.

His sweat-soaked undershirt and Gallant's fast reaction saved his life, but not his beard or patches of his skin. The blanket grabbed swiftly from the bunk by Gallant and flung like a matador's swirling cape enveloped Arkle's head and shoulders, suffocating the flames and muffling the bartender's screams. But the burning oil had splashed indiscriminately. The dry timber of the door was already alight, and the frantic slapping of Arkle's hands had sprayed burning fuel on to the net curtains. As those caught, the flames licked upwards. In the space of seconds it became clear to Gallant that Danson's house was doomed: they had to get out, and fast.

Again Melody Lake was ahead of him. With Arkle still thrashing around in the folds of the blanket she ran at him and pushed him bodily with her out of the now burning building. He fell flat on his back, twisted, and began to crawl blindly away. Then Gallant was outside, limping, singed, coughing – but alive. He and Melody grabbed an arm apiece and dragged Arkle out across the trail to rough grass and the sounds of the creek. Dumped him. Turned to watch as flames flared and a shower of sparks burst through the collapsing roof and whirled into the night skies.

'Salvation Creek,' Melody mused, dark eyes reflecting the dancing flames, 'won't have a fire service.'

'Salvation Creek,' Gallant said, 'won't have any interest. The house stands on its own, and is no danger to others – though more's the pity. It will burn, die, and quickly be forgotten.'

'Then let's take this nasty little man home. Home being the Last Chance – right?'

'Right, somewhere where he can deaden the pain by imbibing strong alcohol in vast quantities,' Gallant said. 'And when we've tossed him through the curtain,' he added, grinning, 'I'll take you to my bedroom where we will spend a comfortable night on beds of straw, soothed by the snoring of two fine horses.'

TWENTY-ONE

Born Gallant and Melody Lake rode into Kansas City at dawn, the cold streets awakening with the coming of light, riders cantering in from nearby ranches, wagons creaking and rumbling towards warehouses and grain stores, aproned shopkeepers and business-men in suits yawning as they opened their premises.

They'd arranged to join Stick McCrae in the Kansas City hotel room where Gallant and the news-paperman had first met several months previously. Or what Gallant thought had been a first meeting. McCrae had been sitting on Gallant's bed when he'd walked in. The newspaperman had a Winchester .73 resting across his thighs. It transpired that they'd had a recent brief encounter in Salvation Creek's Last Chance saloon, where McCrae – playing a part but looking for news – had suggested to Gallant that if he wanted milk he should go to Millie's dairy. Instead, Gallant had downed strong liquor, ignored the menace of Sundown Tancred and broken the jaw of a man by the name of Wilson Teager.

The doors of the hotel where he retained that room were permanently open. Gallant, always the gentleman, let Lake precede him, told her the room number, and they climbed two flights of bare wooden stairs. McCrae was waiting on a gloomy landing. He had been up early, had watched their arrival through the window overlooking the street.

He looked amused, but tense.

'You've got straw in your hair.'

Melody scowled. 'Blame what Gallant calls his bedroom.'

'Smelly, but warm,' Gallant said. 'Actually, don't you know, that's a spitting description for Jake Arkle after Danson's house went up in flames.'

'You can tell me about that later,' McCrae said, stepping aside to let them past, then shutting the door. 'Right now we have problems.'

'Brush them aside, treat them with contempt,' Melody said. 'My first stop is Ed Grant's office, and with the requisite, incriminating documents in my hot little hand it's then away with all speed to the offices of Judge . . . damn, d'you know, I've forgotten his name!'

'In the circumstances,' McCrae said, 'that's the least of our worries.'

'Oh hell,' Melody said, meeting his gaze. 'What's going on, Stick?'

'Ed's office was burgled. Turned over. Filing cabinets opened and emptied. Also, the thieves knew the safe's combination. It was wide open.'

'When?'

'Yesterday,' McCrae said.

'And those incriminating documents gone? Well, yes, they would be, wouldn't they, because that's what they were after. Without them, I've got nothing – dammit, I need them to have any hope of bringing down Emerson Judd.'

'An office so completely ransacked,' Gallant said, 'tells us something about the robbers. It suggests the search became more desperate by the minute. Maybe that was because Judd's ruffians couldn't find what they were looking for.'

'That sounds suspiciously like a blue-blooded optimist clutching at straws,' Melody said, 'but, yes, any port in a storm, or some such metaphor. For the truth, we go and talk to Ed.'

'You don't, but I do,' Gallant said. 'I want Stick to go to those offices where sweaty men wear sleeve garters and green eye shades, see what they know about the robbery.'

'The news came from there, from a man I trust,' McCrae said.

'Then talk to him face to face, get him to spill anything he didn't put into print. Melody, you should go and talk to the judge with no name, let him know all is not lost.'

'Before, having heard the news, he crosses my name out of his court diary and heads imperiously away to pass judgement somewhere where lawyers are more competent. Yes, you're right, I'll do that.

147

Soften him in some way, possibly by gently stroking his wig.'

'It's probably gathering moths in a dusty drawer,' Gallant said.

'And anyway,' McCrae said, 'before you set sail and at the risk of adding to your grief. . .'

'Forget about grief. Granddad and I were like all very young and very old, affectionate, but distant. If sadness comes at all, it'll be when I'm done with Emerson Judd so, go on.'

McCrae's smile was sympathetic, his eyes bleak.

'I learnt more about the passing of your grandfather, Frank Lake, much of it confirming what Gallant and I had already worked out. Your kidnapping got your grandpa into a tangled web of intrigue. He saved your life by abandoning cherished principles and aligning himself with Judd. His bringing Gallant into the picture in Salvation Creek came about because he discovered it was Emerson Judd who ordered the killing of his son – your father – and all deals were off. Sadly, by bringing Gallant in he was effectively ending his own life, and leaving his granddaughter's hanging by a slender thread.'

'Which means,' Melody Lake said, 'that more than ever we need to know what's happened to those documents, and I'm wondering why Gallant's still sitting here with his mouth open.'

'Strange that we've not mentioned that tough-as-nails black hat, Chet Eagan,' Gallant said, frowning.

'Well now you have,' Melody said. 'Does he bother you?'

'Odds on he was in on that Ed Grant robbery,' Gallant said. 'If I'm right and he didn't find those documents, the easy option they've always had, which we've tactfully avoided mentionin', is still the best.'

'Killing Melody,' Stick said softly, 'is best even if every one of those documents has been taken, and reduced to ashes. Kill her, and it's over. So to hell with newspaper offices and men with green eye shades. I go with our feisty lawyer, ride shotgun. If Chet Eagan wants her out of the game, he'll quickly find he's bitten off more than he can chew.'

TWENTY-TWO

Born Gallant found Ed Grant surveying the ruins of his office, the tall, lean Pinkerton investigator justifiably furious. It transpired that the burglars had wreaked havoc unnecessarily. Melody Lake's documents were long gone. Grant had anticipated just such a move by Emerson Judd, had packed the documents in his saddle-bags and, late one night, taken them elsewhere.

Where elsewhere? Gallant had politely enquired.

Although the question had been unnecessary, because there was, surely, but one logical place of safety.

And so, less than an hour after leaving Stick McCrae and Melody Lake, Born Gallant was once again in the saddle, pushing his roan hard towards the south-east. In that direction lay Salvation Creek. And so too, but much closer, did the property and the ranch house owned by the late Frank Lake.

Trouble was, Gallant was already playing catch-up,

because even black-hat Chet Eagan was capable of putting two and two together and arriving at the correct answer.

TWENTY-THREE

It comes down to this, Gallant thought, on leaving Kansas City. Just me, and Chet Eagan. Again. Two grown men fighting like schoolboy savages over something that is not our concern.

So if it was to end on the Lake spread, what the hell had been the point of that long ride to El Dorado? The distance covered, back in England, would have taken him all the way south from London to the English Channel. After leaving Salvation Creek, in the cold of more than one moonlit night, he had killed men; unnecessarily, as it turned out, because the young woman he had been sent to rescue had escaped captivity before he reached her crude prison, and done it with an ease that defied belief.

In the miserable chill of that wet night, she had waited in the woods for Gallant and Stick McCrae. When they rode up tensely discussing her fate she had emerged to mock them in that amused, sardonic tone so familiar to Gallant. But, there, didn't that say

152

it all? Gallant knew now he could have stayed in Kansas City, McCrae in Dodge, and on that same night Melody Lake would have conked her guard on the head, stolen his ragged pony and ridden north without any need to wait for two unwanted heroes.

Daylight in country as flat as Kansas was not the best of times to ride up on an exposed ranch house almost certainly harbouring a hired gunman on a mission. One storey, wider than it was deep, the house had a full-length gallery and was set back fully half a mile from the track that snaked away towards Salvation Creek. A scattering of barns around a dusty yard gave any watcher a choice of hiding places.

No stout gateposts or fancy high board marked the entrance to the property with arrogance, for this place had been owned by a decent working man and his devoted wife. From the crosspiece of a post like a miniature gibbet hung a board bearing the name: Lake. But where Gallant might have expected stands of tall trees planted down the long approach to break up the raw prevailing winds, there was nothing. No cover of any kind.

And what kind of a fool am I going to look, Gallant mused, *riding down there clinging to my horse like a bally Indian brave, adopting a zigzag course to foil the man's aim when all he has to do is wait by the window in the jolly old living room and watch my antics.*

But those thoughts were dismissed with a shake of the head, for Gallant was already walking the roan off the trail on to the rutted track now sprouting grass, then kicking it into a canter with his heels and making damn sure he rode erect in the saddle. That wind, never absent, had flipped his flat black hat from his head to hang on shoulders brushed by streaming blond hair allowed to grow long.

If Melody Lake could have seen him, she would surely have approved of his magnificent insouciance. But of interested onlookers there was only the one, and for Gallant that man had nothing but contempt.

The first shot came when Gallant was fifty yards out. The muzzle flashed red where he'd expected it, in one of the house's front windows. Fired from a six-gun, with commendable accuracy, the bullet kicked up dust between the roan's forelegs. It snorted in disdain.

The second bullet chipped splinters from the hitch rail when Gallant was out of the saddle and tethering the roan. The third split the dry boards between his boots when he was crossing the gallery. The fourth. . .

The fourth shot went unfired, the brass cartridge nestling in the chamber beneath the cocked hammer of Chet Eagan's six-gun when Gallant kicked open the front door and walked into the dim front room. The man was sitting by the window. Gun levelled. Elbows on the table. His teeth bared in a mocking grin. Same mildewed black hat as opposed to his brother's preferred off-white. Same all-black outfit first seen by Gallant in Wichita's Buckhorn saloon, now more faded and worn. If he were to look closely, Gallant supposed, he would see scars where he, Gallant, had torn away most of the man's scalp in a spray of blood. But that close look, he imagined, would be possible only if or when the man was dead.

'No fancy talk?' Eagan said. 'None of that damn fool English spiel you believe distracts those stupid enough to listen?'

'There's a time and a place. This ain't it.'

Gallant was grinning. Another distraction? He took a step into the room, nodded at the manila folder by Eagan's elbow.

'Very decent of you, findin' those valuable documents for me.'

'Ten minutes later,' Eagan said, 'you'd have found nothing but ashes.'

'Bein' late's not one of my bad habits,' Gallant said, and he put his weight on one leg and with the other kicked the table out from under Chet Eagan.

Still clutched in Eagan's fist, the gun hit the floor hard as the outlaw went down. The impact tripped the sear, dropped the hammer. The muzzle flashed, the bullet thumped into the back of a low settee. Stuffing flew like grey dust. Eagan's head had also made hard contact with the floor. He was on his back under the splintered table, kicking feebly. Gallant stepped in, swept up the fallen manila folder and tossed it out through the open front door.

Another wild kick, stronger as Eagan recovered, sent the table flying. The top's thin edge hit Gallant below the knee like the blade of an axe. His leg collapsed. Down on his other knee, he fell sideways in a blur of pain. His hand flashed to his Peacemaker.

Tugged. The gun snagged in the holster. Six feet away, Eagan rolled, snapped a shot. The bullet shattered a hanging oil lamp. Coal oil splashed Gallant's face. He spat, wrenched his six-gun free. Eagan had slithered away on his back. Now he was halfway up, neck and shoulders supported by the edge of the settee's seat. Steadier, the next shot was well placed, ripping the Peacemaker from Gallant's hand. The next. . . .

The next was the seventh shot from a six-gun, which made it nothing more than the metallic click of hammer on empty chamber. Furious clicking convinced Eagan the gun wasn't misfiring. He cursed, threw the useless weapon at Gallant, followed it with a kick that sliced harmlessly through thin air; struggled to rise so that he could launch himself at Gallant.

But being late, Gallant had said, was not one of his bad habits.

Ignoring the dropped Peacemaker, his bleeding knuckles, he pounced cat-like on Eagan before the outlaw had his legs under him. He drove him down hard. It flashed through Gallant's mind – a faint hope – that the edge of the settee might snap the outlaw's neck. But the years had worn the cushions as soft and slippery as wet moss. Eagan slid without harm, flopped, rolled clear. He twisted, hammered a vicious side-fist blow at Gallant's head. Gallant took it on the side of his skull, saw stars flashing, fell back and aimed a kick at Eagan's head.

With the speed of a man swatting at flies, Eagan

caught Gallant's ankle in his big fist. Squeezed, dragged Gallant across the floor. Gallant went with the pull. Eagan had hold of his bullet-bruised ankle. Pain was painting the room with red mist. He felt Eagan come up off the floor, keep hold of the bruised ankle, lift that leg high.

The kick aimed at the exposed fork of Gallant's legs was intended to finish the aristocratic Englishman, but the intense pain of knee and ankle now served to sharpen Gallant's reactions. He saw the kick coming as if in slow motion. With precise timing he ripped his ankle from Eagan's grip and turned the sole of his boot towards the man's advancing shin. Thin bone met hard leather. The man roared in pain, lifted his knee, grabbed his leg. Knew at once that the situation had been reversed, and tried desperately to recover.

Too late.

Gallant's kick, from the floor, took Eagan between the legs. The outlaw went down on his knees doubled up, and vomited profusely into his own black-clad lap.

All that could be heard, in that sudden, aching silence – well, aching more for Chet Eagan, Gallant thought – was the ticking of Ellis Lake's old longcase clock. Then, from a far distance, came the faint sound of fast-approaching hoofbeats.

EPILOGUE

'I'm a newspaperman,' McCrae said over celebratory drinks. 'Back in Dodge I'll make sure this gets in the paper, a story that pulls no punches and puts credit where credit's due.'

'You've got a headline all worked out?' Gallant said.

'Damn right I have. *The Eldorado Sojourn.* Sounds innocent enough, but then there's a sub-heading that will intrigue readers: *How a pleasant vacation in a woodland cabin gave a young lawyer the strength to bring a corrupt politician to his knees.*

Melody Lake was flushed, but smiling. 'Don't tell your editor to hold the front page just yet, Stick. The hearing's some days away – and I could lose.'

'You'll win,' McCrae said, in a tone that brooked no argument.

Not that they had any. Melody, Gallant knew, was simply being modest. She was supremely confident, and driven: in a roundabout way, but there nonetheless, her grandfather's death was on her conscience.

She did win her courtroom battle, and without judge or jurors having to indulge in any long deliberations. The incriminating documents held by Ed Grant of Pinkertons, then by Frank Lake – then, briefly, by the now jailed Chet Eagan – told a story of corruption in high places. Emerson Judd walked out of the courtroom without shackles, but he was a beaten man. He never again held public office.